TOP COW PRODUCTIONS PRESENTS

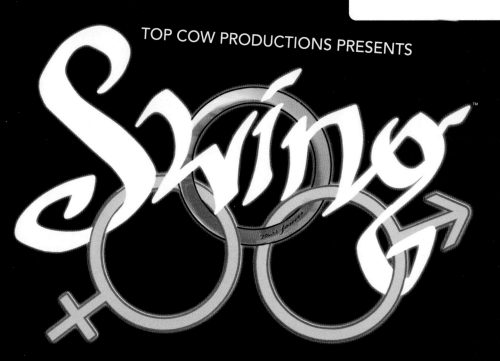

Created by

LINDA SEJIC, MATT HAWKINS & JENNI CHEUNG

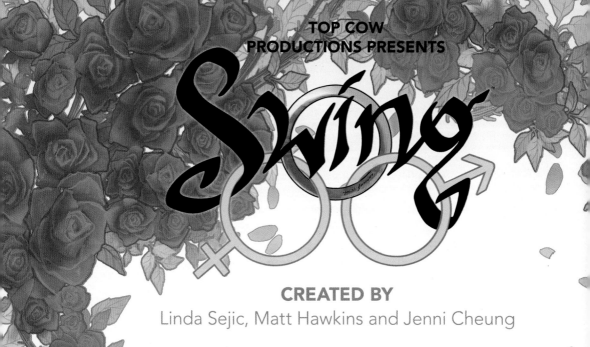

TOP COW
PRODUCTIONS PRESENTS

Swing

CREATED BY
Linda Sejic, Matt Hawkins and Jenni Cheung

WRITTEN BY
Matt Hawkins
Jenni Cheung

ART AND LETTERING
Linda Sejic

**BASED ON A STORY
AND CHARACTERS DEVELOPED BY**
Linda Sejic
Stjepan Sejic
Matt Hawkins
Jenni Cheung

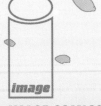

IMAGE COMICS, INC.
Robert Kirkman – Chief Operating Officer
Erik Larsen – Chief Financial Officer
Todd McFarlane – President
Marc Silvestri – Chief Executive Officer
Jim Valentino – Vice President
Eric Stephenson – Publisher / Chief Creative Officer
Corey Hart – Director of Sales
Jeff Boison – Director of Publishing Planning & Book Trade Sales
Chris Ross – Director of Digital Sales
Jeff Stang – Director of Specialty Sales
Kat Salazar – Director of PR & Marketing
Drew Gill – Art Director
Heather Doornink – Production Director
Nicole Lapalme – Controller
IMAGECOMICS.COM

"INTO THE LIFESTYLE"

We make arrangements to meet at local trendy LA bar. We show up on time and get a drink while we wait. We are almost ready to leave as they come in 45 minutes late. They are in their early 20s a few years out of college where they met. She is 5'5" with an infectious smile and dyed-blonde hair like honey wheat. So let's call her Honey. Not my usual type, but pretty with an outgoing personality. He is a laid-back soccer player 5'10", so we'll call him Dave. For reference, I'm 6'1", fit, with salt and pepper hair, and my girlfriend Lilly is a dark-haired beauty in her early 30s with curves in all the right places. They get drinks, Jameson and a screwdriver, then settle in to chat about the innocuous details of our lives, and how we are all new to this.

After an hour we decide to take a field trip to a sex shop down the street to look for an outfit for a party we are attending the next weekend. It's a good icebreaker. We buy some sexy things and decide to go back to our place for a lingerie show. Once in our room Dave and I sit on the bed while the girls model. Honey, with a wicked grin, starts to kiss my girlfriend then pushes her on top of me and starts going down. She invites her man in for a taste and I see Lilly's eyes roll back as I caress her face and two heads pleasure her. After a bit they trade places and Lilly goes down on the blonde while fondling her boyfriend.

Honey comes over to me and we start kissing. She is biting my neck and grinding into my lap. Things start to get hot as all the clothes come off. We begin with our own partners. I have my girl doggie so she can watch this cute blonde ride her man. The girls decide to change partners and start to give side by side blow jobs like it's a race. It's good, but my girl has no gag reflex and actually, I am proud to share her skills. He looks like she is sucking his soul out. I ask if we should continue and all are enthusiastic at the prospect.

I open a new box of condoms and hand him one. He wastes no time and in his eagerness puts it on inside out and apologizes for wasting it. We have a whole box! I am still getting head, but look down and ask if she is ready as I hold a blue packet between my fingers. It is on!

I ask how she wants it and she says "doggie" as she flips to all fours. I position myself and press in, slowly picking up speed. I look over and see him pounding my girl. I remember being that young, crushing like it's your last meal. I fuck for some time, putting down torque as both girls moan in stereo. She is wet and I adjust because she is a bit taller so I can fuck her hard. I make eye contact with Lilly and we smile at each other for being naughty.

The positions change; he goes doggie and I lay Honey on her back. I kiss her neck and pull her into me. She is sweating hard now while kissing me then tonguing my ear which turns me on. I pull out and go down on her again as she encourages her man to fuck my girl doggie so she can watch. She moans and writhes as I eat her out. I am distracted for a moment as I hear a freight train pounding my girlfriend to orgasm.

The action ends with sweaty bodies and soiled sheets. We pull the linens and shower. It's past 3AM. We say our goodbyes and look forward to the next encounter. I felt 99% good and 1% jealous. I figure that was good, because if I didn't feel anything I'm a sociopath and if I was too jealous it would not work. In the end she is still mine and I hers. We had this experience together.

This was our first swap and entry into "lifestyle," two years ago this week. We started with a threesome and met a couple where we played in the same room with some touching, but this was the first hard swap from Adam's perspective. It went great, but we didn't hear from them after and when we checked in, we learned they were friends with benefits and there was some jealousy with Honey seeing him with another girl like that. Lesson learned.

When people hear the word "swinger," they usually think indiscriminate orgies, seedy 70s key parties or kinky masquerades rolled up with paddling. Elements of these do have their place, but "lifestyle" encompasses so much more!

KEY TERMS

LIFESTYLE	The Swinger Ethos.
FULL SWAP	Intercourse with another partner.
SOFT SWAP	The widest and most confusing term. Any contact with other partners from touching up to oral sex stopping short of intercourse (good idea to discuss with potential partners).
HALL PASS	A partner in a couple can play alone.
UNICORN	Single girl who plays with couples.
VANILLA	All the people not in lifestyle.
BDSM	Bondage, discipline, dominance and submission.
POLYAMORY	Relationships with other partners. More than just friends with benefits

Lifestyle is certainly not for everyone and requires a high level of trust, confidence and communication to do successfully. If you are a single girl, it's all a bit different and single guys do exist, but it is more of a rarity. Understanding your desires and boundaries and managing potential jealousy are the keys to good experiences. People want various experiences. For some it is just about the sex. Others want deep friendships with benefits. People may be into multiple partners, orgies, voyeurism exhibitionism or exploring BDSM. It may be a platitude, but it is what you make it.

We like that people are friendly and like-minded in the lifestyle. When you go to a Vanilla party or club, people are usually guarded, staring at phones and hard to talk to. Lifestyle events tend to be very social and people are more inclusive. Girls are super friendly and guys rarely creepily stare and will not touch you without consent. We have had some very sexy fun and met some amazing people we consider close friends. Actually, the funny thing is the friends have been the best part for us. Who else can you share naked vacation photos with?

There is also the wild, crazy, mind-blowing sex!!! Lilly says, "For me as a woman, there's nothing hotter than to see my man enjoy himself. In a way, it's like watching great porn with your favorite man as the lead!" Sex as a team sport can be unbelievable! Chess instead of checkers, more combinations, greater possibilities. You explore your fantasy to understand what you like may be different from what you thought you liked. We have had 15 naked people in a hot tub. Played "find your girl" by identifying her breasts, but only using your mouth. Two words – Naked Twister!

Here are a few suggested rules of the road that work for us: **1)** Women are in charge. They usually instigate and drive the play, particularly with new partners. **2)** Guys need to be respectful and ask permission! **3)** Know your boundaries and understand those of the people you play with. **4)** Don't take one for the team. If you are not attracted to someone, wait and find a situation everyone is excited to explore. **5)** Trust instincts, if something seems amiss, it probably is. **6)** Lifestyle can enhance a relationship, but it won't fix one that's not working.

Get tested regularly and play safe! Health and safety are always our top priorities. No one wants to get an STD or give one. This is like regular dating and not everyone is conscientious. This is an adult sport so you need to act like it, discuss it openly and take the proper precautions. Good prospects should have the same concerns and priorities as you do.

Make good choices and have fun!

ADAM & LILLY

CAST

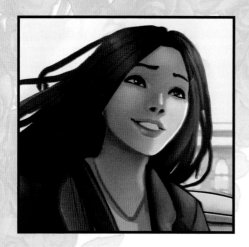

Cathy Chang

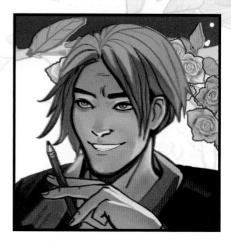

Dan Lincoln

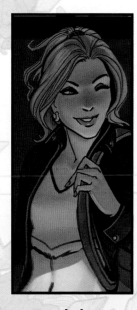

Debbie
Wildes

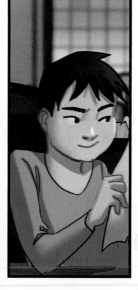

Blake
Lincoln

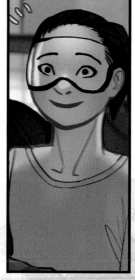

Ashley
Lincoln

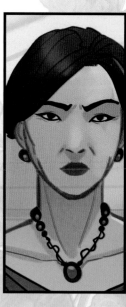

Mom

CHAPTER ONE

EVERYTHING SEEMED SO BRIGHT BACK THEN.
INTERESTING.
NEW.
LIFE WAS FULL OF ADVENTUROUS NEW EXPERIENCES AND ENDLESS POSSIBILITIES.
CATHY, COULD YOU STOP DAYDREAMING FOR FIVE MINUTES AND COME HELP?
WELL...NEARLY ENDLESS.

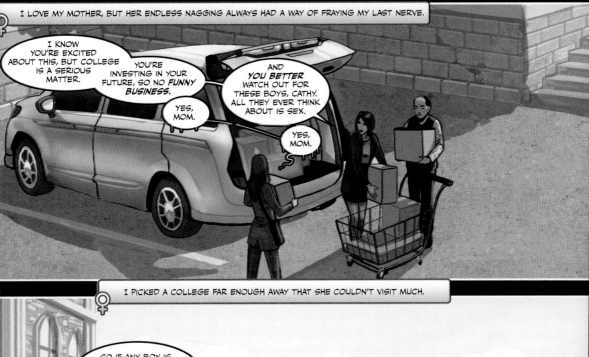

I LOVE MY MOTHER, BUT HER ENDLESS NAGGING ALWAYS HAD A WAY OF FRAYING MY LAST NERVE.

I KNOW YOU'RE EXCITED ABOUT THIS, BUT COLLEGE IS A SERIOUS MATTER.

YOU'RE INVESTING IN YOUR FUTURE, SO NO *FUNNY BUSINESS.*

YES, MOM.

AND *YOU BETTER* WATCH OUT FOR THESE BOYS, CATHY. ALL THEY EVER THINK ABOUT IS SEX.

YES, MOM.

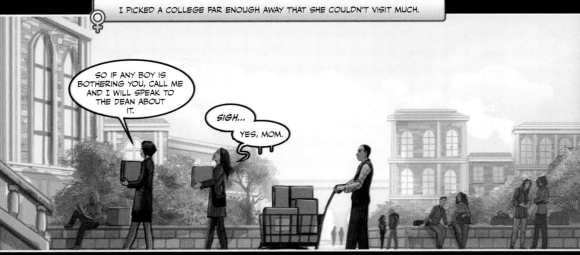

I PICKED A COLLEGE FAR ENOUGH AWAY THAT SHE COULDN'T VISIT MUCH.

SO IF ANY BOY IS BOTHERING YOU, CALL ME AND I WILL SPEAK TO THE DEAN ABOUT IT.

SIGH... YES, MOM.

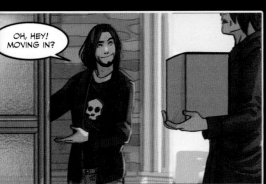

OH, HEY! MOVING IN?

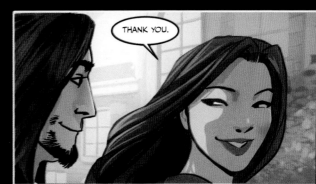

THANK YOU.

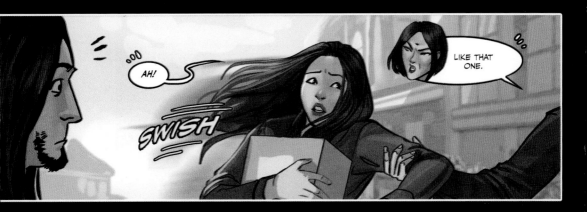

AH!

SWISH

LIKE THAT ONE.

DAD, HELP!
MY FATHER AND I SHARED THE SAME FATE...
SIGH...
SO I KNEW I COULD ALWAYS COUNT ON HIS SUPPORT.
BACK THEN, I ENVIED HIS SEEMINGLY ENDLESS PATIENCE.
CATHY, WHICH ROOM NUMBER WAS IT AGAIN?
BUT IT ALL CHANGED AFTER I LEFT.
AH! ONE SEC. LEMME CHECK.
OH, HEY!
I THINK WE'RE HERE!
MY OTHER STUFF

CONTRARY TO MY MOTHER'S ADVICE, AT THE TIME I WAS MORE INTERESTED IN BOYS THAN STUDYING.
UGH, COME ON! I KNOW I PACKED YOU!
YESSS!
BUT IT WAS STILL HARD TO SHAKE OFF SOME OF THE GOOD GIRL INDOCTRINATION I'D GATHERED OVER THE YEARS.
SWISH
HEY, LEAVE HIM UP! HE'S KINDA CUTE!
CLACK
I GUESS, IN THE END, ALL I NEEDED WAS THE RIGHT KIND OF INFLUENCE.
OR THE WRONG KIND!

MY ROOMMATE *DEBBIE* CONTRIBUTED TO MY "MORAL DECLINE" -- (MY MOTHER'S WORDS, NOT MINE).

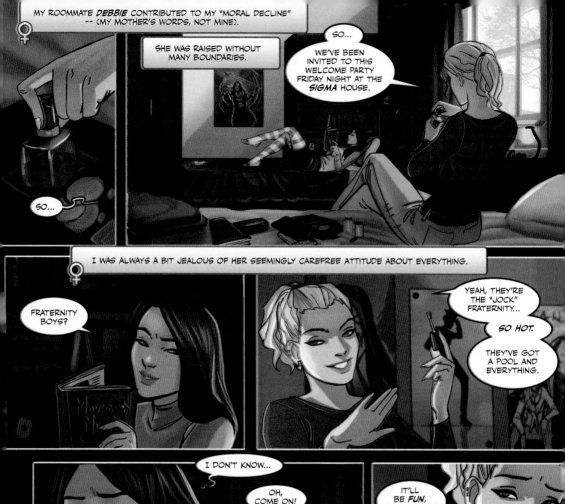

SHE WAS RAISED WITHOUT MANY BOUNDARIES.

SO...

WE'VE BEEN INVITED TO THIS WELCOME PARTY FRIDAY NIGHT AT THE *SIGMA* HOUSE.

SO...

I WAS ALWAYS A BIT JEALOUS OF HER SEEMINGLY CAREFREE ATTITUDE ABOUT EVERYTHING.

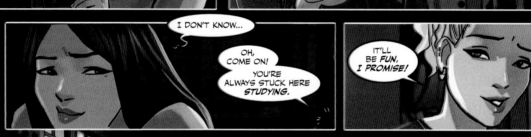

FRATERNITY BOYS?

YEAH, THEY'RE THE "JOCK" FRATERNITY...

SO HOT.

THEY'VE GOT A POOL AND EVERYTHING.

I DON'T KNOW...

OH, COME ON! YOU'RE ALWAYS STUCK HERE *STUDYING.*

IT'LL BE *FUN,* I PROMISE!

SIGMA HOUSE. 10:00 p.m.

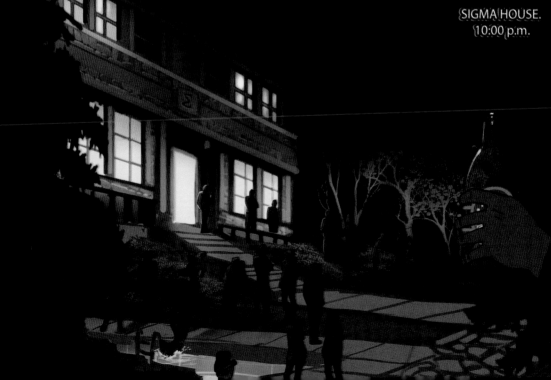

TO DEBBIE, A FRAT PARTY WAS A HUNTING GROUND.
GLUG
GLUG
GLUG
TO ME?
SOOO...
WHAT'S YOUR MAJOR?
UH... I DUNNO.
GLUG
GLUG
GLUG
NOT SO MUCH.
BORED
SIGH...
I NEEDED SOME *ROMANCE* WITH MY SEX!

I ALLOW ONE REWRITE, WHICH CAN BRING YOUR GRADE UP ONE FULL LETTER.
IF YOU'RE INTERESTED, I RECOMMEND YOU VISIT ONE OF MY TAS DURING THEIR POSTED OFFICE HOURS TO DISCUSS HOW TO IMPROVE YOUR PAPER.
COLLEGE WAS WAY HARDER THAN HIGH SCHOOL... AND MY PARENTS WERE PAYING FOR EVERYTHING.
CHAUCER'S CANTERBURY TALES
BY CATHY CHANG.
C+
BAD GRADES MEANT RELOCATING TO A COLLEGE CLOSE ENOUGH TO LIVE AT HOME...
...AND I *DID NOT WANT THAT.*
OFFICE
HELLO?
COME IN!
HI. I'D LIKE TO TALK TO YOU ABOUT MY PAPER. PLANNING TO DO THE REWRITE.
THAT'S HOW I MET DAN.
SURE, HAVE A SEAT.

HE WAS PRETENTIOUS, BUT SMART...ENGAGING.
YEAH, I GRADED THIS ONE.
YOU'VE GOT ALL OF THE FUNDAMENTALS HERE, BUT IT LACKS PASSION.
CHAUCER IS THE FATHER OF ENGLISH POETRY.
HE WAS THE FIRST TO UNDERSTAND MODERN TASTES AND EXPRESSED THE HOPES AND ASPIRATIONS OF THE PEOPLE OF HIS TIME.
CERTAINLY MORE INTERESTING THAN THE UNDERGRAD FRATERNITY BOYS I'D MET.
AND WHAT WERE THEY?
WHAT WERE *WHAT?*
THE HOPES AND ASPIRATIONS OF THE TIME.
WELL... THAT WOULD REQUIRE A WHOLE DISSERTATION, BUT I'VE ALWAYS FOUND HIS TAKE ON SEX, ADULTERY, RELATIONSHIPS, WOMEN, AND LOVE TO BE VERY INTERESTING.
AND YES...ALSO *HOT.*
HITTING ON THE CO-EDS AGAIN, DAN?

NO, SIR.... UH, I WAS TALKING TO HER ABOUT CHAUCER. HER...REWRITE.
AHH, CHAUCER. MISOGYNY, CUCKOLDING, AND ALL KINDS OF INSANITY FROM THAT ERA.
DON'T LET HIM SELL IT TOO HARD AS ROMANCE. IT'S A RELIC OF ITS ERA, BUT WOW DID CHAUCER HATE WOMEN.
HOW CAN YOU SAY THAT? IT'S NOT THAT SIMPLE.
FEMINISM DIDN'T EVEN EXIST THEN!
WOMEN WERE LOOKED AT AS OBJECTS AND YET HE SAW THEM AS MORE THAN THAT BLAH BLAH
BLAH BLAH BLAH BLAH BLAH BLAHBLAH BLAH BLAH BLAH
BLAH BLAH BLAH BLAH BLAH BLAH BLAHBLAH BLAH BLAHBL
BLAH BLAH BLAH BLAH BLAH BLAH BLAH BLAH BLAH BLAH BLAH
BLAH BLAH BLAH BLAH BLAH BLAH BLAHBLAH BLAH BLAHBLA
BLAH BLAH BLAH BLAH BLAHBLAH BLAH BLAHBLAH BLAH BLAH
WATCHING THESE TWO FIGHT OVER THE WORDS A MAN WROTE FIVE HUNDRED-PLUS YEARS AGO MADE ME REALIZE WHAT I HAVE NEVER REALLY HAD IN MY LIFE...

...PASSION.
poetry
YEAH, COME BY DURING OFFICE HOURS AND WE CAN TALK MORE.
I CAN'T WAIT TO HEAR --
HI, DAN!
OH, HEY, CATHY ISN'T IT?
YEAH. I WAS HOPING WE COULD TALK MORE ABOUT CHAUCER...
SURE, JUST COME BY OFFICE HOURS.
...OVER DINNER. MY TREAT.
poetry

SO I'M ALMOST FINISHED WITH MY NOVEL, BEEN WORKING ON IT FOR THE PAST TWO YEARS. I CAN'T WAIT TO GET IT PUBLISHED.
THAT'S SO EXCITING.
THIS IS FUN. YOU'RE SO EASY TO TALK TO!
TO YOU HAVING A GREAT FAKE ID.
TO PEOPLE NOT BEING ABLE TO TELL HOW OLD ASIAN GIRLS ARE.
HA HA HA HA HA HA HA HA

AND THAT'S WHEN IT ALL STARTED...
HEY, WHERE ARE YOU GOING SO EARLY???
IT'S A SECRET.
BUMP!!
MEET ME LATER!!
January
1 MISSED CALLS
MOM
February
OMG, JUST TELL ME!!
ON A SCALE FROM 1 TO 10!!
10!
HE'S SMART, TOO.
OFFICE
CLACK!..
CLICK!
March
4 MISSED CALLS
MOM

2 MISSED CALLS
MOM
April
May
OMG, MOM WE TALKED 3 DAYS AGO...
I'M BUSY!! I'LL CALL YOU BACK WHEN I HAVE THE CHANCE.
June
UH...NO MRS. CHANG, SHE'S NOT HERE NOW, SHE HAS CLASSES...
UH-HUH... EVEN ON SUNDAY... SHE...STUDIES IN THE LIBRARY...

July
2 MISSED CALLS
MOM
WHAT...CATHY?
WHY...YES, O-OF COURSE SHE'S HERE, BUT...SHE'S... UH...ASLEEP.
SHE HAS A REALLY TOUGH TEST TOMORROW, SO...UH... BETTER LET HER REST.
WOW NOT EVEN *YOUR MOM* CALLS YOU *THAT OFTEN.*
HUSH, YOU.

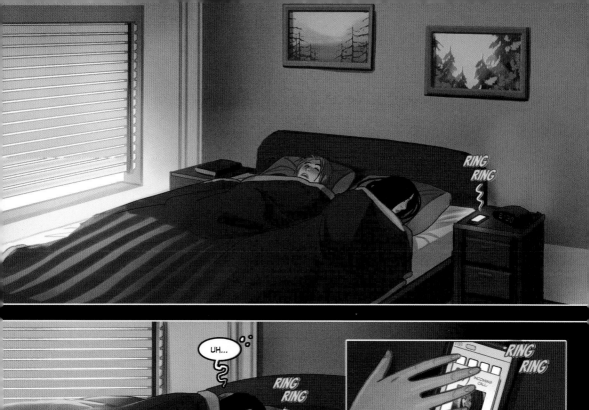

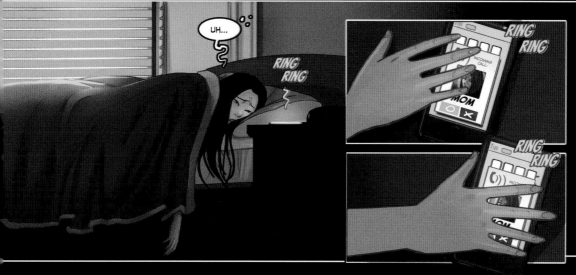

UH...

RING RING

RING RING

RING RING

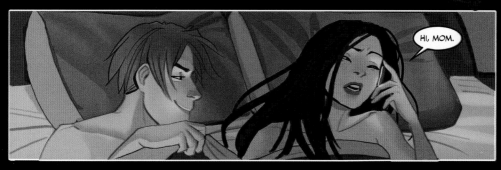

HI, MOM.

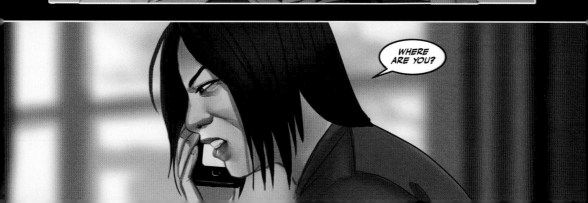

WHERE ARE YOU?

I'M IN THE DORM, MOM.
I DON'T HAVE CLASS TODAY UNTIL 10.
OH, YOU'RE IN YOUR DORM ROOM NOW? THAT'S INTERESTING...
WHY -- DO YOU SAY THAT?
BECAUSE ***I'M*** STANDING IN YOUR DORM ROOM RIGHT NOW.
AND YOUR ROOMMATE TOLD ME THAT YOU'RE OFF WITH YOUR ***BOYFRIEND.***
I'M SORRY, CATH...
SHE IS REALLY INTIMIDATING FACE-TO-FACE...AND I...RAN OUT OF EXCUSES.
I'LL BE RIGHT THERE!!

STOP IT!
SIGH...
WHAT IS IT?
I GUESS IT'S TIME TO MEET *MY PARENTS.*

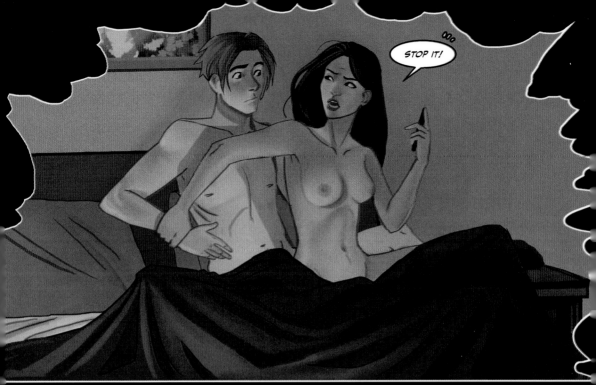

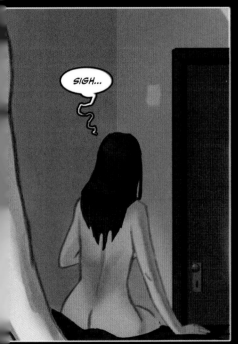

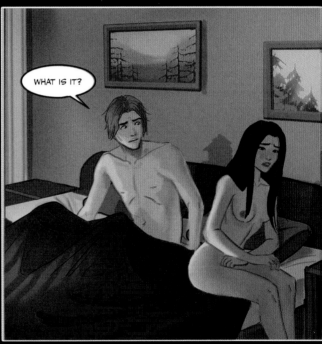

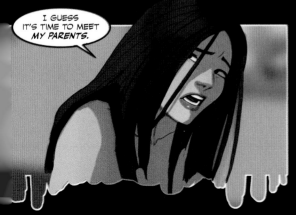

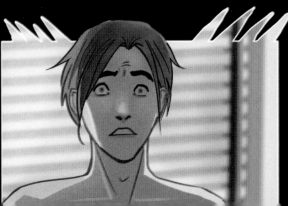

這次又有什麼新花樣?
媽咪, 他是我的男朋友。
<DAN IS WORKING ON HIS POSTDOC IN ENGLISH LITERATURE. HE'S WRITING A NOVEL. HE'S A WRITER.>
<YOU COULDN'T FIND A DOCTOR OR A LAWYER? SOMEONE WITH A MORE STABLE CAREER?
IT'S BAD ENOUGH HE'S WHITE, BUT A ***WRITER?***
YOUR SECOND COUSIN MARRIED A WHITE WRITER AND NOW THEY LIVE IN A TRAILER PARK.>
POKE
POKE
<I LOVE HIM. THAT SHOULD BE ENOUGH.>
<CATHY!>
<WHY CAN'T YOU SUPPORT THE ONE THING I WANT FOR MYSELF?>
<I'VE ALWAYS DONE EVERYTHING YOU ASKED OF ME. I'VE BEEN A GOOD DAUGHTER. I'M AN ADULT NOW, LET ME CHOOSE SOMETHING FOR MYSELF.>

‹OKAY.
IT'S HARD TO SEE MY ONLY DAUGHTER BECOME A WOMAN.›
‹IF YOU LOVE HIM, I WILL TRY AND ACCEPT HIM.›
‹OH, THANK YOU, MOM!!
THANK YOU! THANK YOU! THANK YOU!!!›
‹JUST DON'T GET PREGNANT.›
WHAT'D SHE SAY?
SHE CAN'T WAIT TO READ YOUR BOOK.

AND THEN...IT WAS ON!

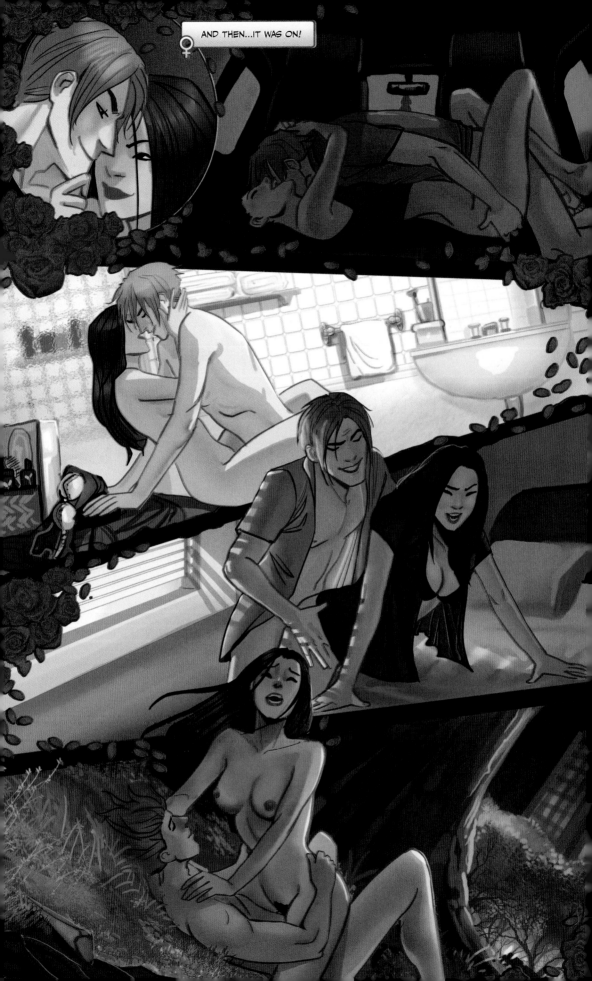

PREGNANT

NOT
PREGNANT

CHAPTER TWO

TAP TAP
TAP TAP
SIGH...
CONTACTS:
CALL DAN?
CONTACTS:
DAN
CANCEL?
RING RING
RING RING
INCOMING CALL:
DAN
RING RING

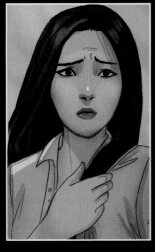
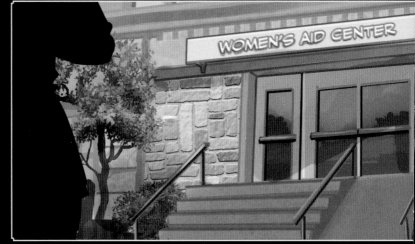
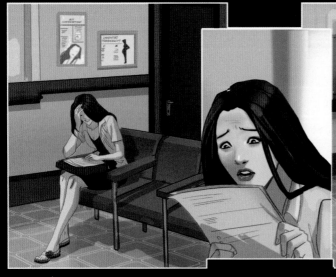
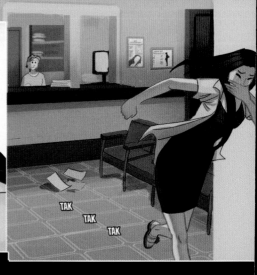

TAK
TAK
TAK

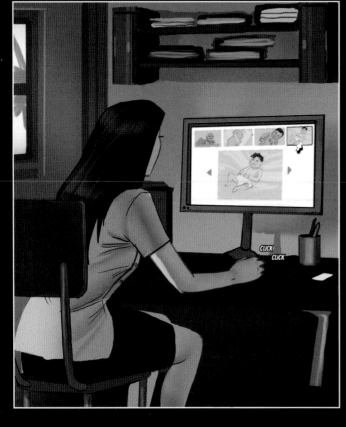

CLICK
CLICK

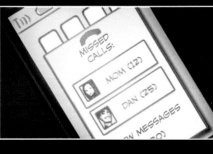

MISSED
CALLS:

MOM (12)

DAN (25)

W MESSAGES

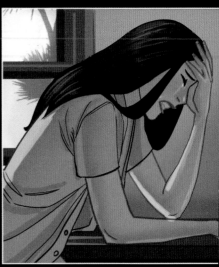

WHAT'S THE MATTER, LOVE? YOU'VE BEEN AVOIDING ME ALL WEEK. ARE YOU BREAKING UP WITH ME?
I'M PREGNANT.
WHAT DO YOU WANT TO DO?
I WENT TO THE CLINIC...TO GET AN ABORTION.
I WASN'T EVEN GOING TO TELL YOU.
BUT I GOT THERE AND COULDN'T DO IT...
I WANTED TO TALK TO YOU.
SEE HOW YOU FELT ABOUT IT.
I DON'T THINK I *WANT* TO GET AN ABORTION.
I'VE NEVER LOVED ANYONE MORE THAN I LOVE YOU, CATH.
WAKING UP NEXT TO YOU EVERY DAY IS A JOY THAT I'D LIKE TO EXPERIENCE EVERY DAY FOR THE REST OF MY LIFE.

I HAVE TO REMIND MYSELF I'M ONLY *TWENTY-SEVEN.*
MOST OF MY HIGH SCHOOL FRIENDS AREN'T EVEN MARRIED YET.
TWO KIDS.
CAREER.
HOMEOWNER.
EIGHT YEARS.
THE TIME HAS REALLY FLOWN BY.

THE KIDS ARE ASLEEP.
I'VE BEEN NEGLECTING DAN LATELY.
WE HAVEN'T HAD SEX IN A WHILE.
TOO...WEIRD.
TOO SLUTTY.
HMMM...

OUR SEX USED TO BE AWESOME.
WE COULD BARELY KEEP OUR HANDS OFF EACH OTHER FOR MORE THAN A DAY OR TWO.
THAT BECAME THREE TIMES A WEEK...
DAN, PLEASE. I'M TIRED.
THEN TWO...
NOT NOW HONEY, THE KIDS ARE STILL UP.
THEN ONE...
PERIOD.
AND SOMETIMES, LONG STRETCHES OF NONE.
RESPONSIBILITY
HE DOESN'T TRY VERY HARD ANYMORE.
HE USED TO AT LEAST PRETEND HE WANTED TO GIVE ME A MASSAGE FIRST AS A SIGNAL HE WANTED SOME.
LIGHTLY KISS MY NECK BEFORE TAKING ME.
LIKE WHAT YOU SEE?
NOW HE JUST WAVES HIS DICK IN MY FACE.

I CAN'T BLAME IT ALL ON HIM THOUGH.
I'VE NOT BEEN VERY RECEPTIVE.
I'VE TURNED DOWN HIS LAST FEW ADVANCES.
SO I'M GOING TO MAKE IT UP TO HIM AND FUCK HIS BRAINS OUT.
HE HAS NO IDEA WHAT'S COMING FOR HIM.

DO IT, ELLY.
ON IT!
SWISH
POK
PIOOO
ALL RIGHT, DAN. THAT'S YOUR 10 SEC INVULNERABILITY, SO GO FIND THE BOSS AND BRING IT HERE.
10 SEC
+ ALL DMG RESIST
+ IMMUNE
9
DUDE, I KNOW, I'VE DONE THIS BEFORE.
8
HMM...
THERE'S NOTHING HERE!
ARE YOU SURE WE'RE IN THE RIGHT ROOM?
RIIGHT... "DONE THIS BEFORE."
SURE.
GUYS, COME ON!
IT'S LATE AND I'M TIRED TOO, BUT WE'VE COME THIS FAR.
HERE, DAN!
MAYBE THIS WILL HELP!
CATCH!

I STILL DON'T SEE IT.
IT'S RIGHT BEHIND YOU!
HEY, LOVER.
AAAAAH!
HEHEHEE
WHAT THE HELL, CATH?
mute

THE KIDS ARE ASLEEP...
...LET'S FUCK!
OK, DAN, YOU HAVE ITS ATTENTION, NOW BRING IT OVER!
HP
I RAID ON TUESDAYS AND THURSDAYS.
YOU KNOW THAT!
DUDE!! MOVE!!! I CAN'T HEAL YOU FROM THERE.
WHAT IS HE DOING?
I'VE NO IDEA.
UGH, FINE, I'M COMING! HANG ON!
ARE YOU CRAZY??
THAT THING'LL SQUISH YOU LIKE A BUG.
IT'S STILL AGGRO'D, MAYBE I CAN MAKE IT.
COME ON.
DON'T YOU LIKE MY OUTFIT?
OH, NOPE!
NEVERMIND, HE'S DOWN!

IT LOOKS NICE, BUT SHOULD YOU BE WALKING AROUND LIKE THAT?
WHAT IF ONE OF THE KIDS WOKE UP?
OH, CRAP! IT'S ON ME NOW!!!!
RUN, ELLY!
I'LL TRY TO DIVERT ITS ATTENTION.
I TRIED TO HAVE SEX WITH YOU TWICE OVER THE WEEKEND AND YOU SAID NO, BUT NOW YOU WANT IT ON MY GAMING NIGHT?
ONE OF THE FEW TIMES I HAVE TO MYSELF?
I'LL TRY TO SLOW IT DOWN.
FREEZE, BASTARD!
HEY!
OVER HERE, UGLY!
OH, HEY! IT STOPPED.
WAIT... NEVERMIND!
THAT ONLY ENRAGED IT!
FUUUCK!
FINE!
THEN ENJOY BEING BY YOURSELF.
YEAHHH... THAT'S A WIPE.
CATH, WAIT!
DAN?
SORRY, GUYS, WI-FI CRAPPED OUT.
UNMUTE
SIGH, LET'S WRAP UP. IT'S LATE ANYWAY.
TOLD YOU I SHOULD'VE TANKED. BUT NOOOOO...

I LOVE MY WIFE *VERY MUCH.*
CLICK
BUT SOMETIMES I DON'T UNDERSTAND HER.
CATH, LET ME IN HONEY, I'M SORRY.
I LOVE MY HUSBAND.
BUT SOMETIMES I JUST DON'T UNDERSTAND HIM.
HE COMPLAINS ABOUT US NOT HAVING SEX --
AND THEN HE BLOWS ME OFF --
POOF!
-- *FOR A VIDEO GAME!*
SLAM

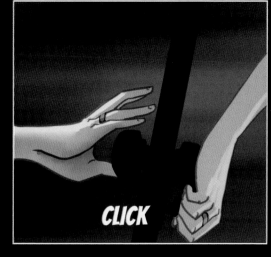

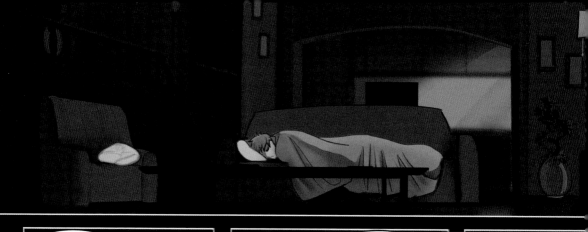

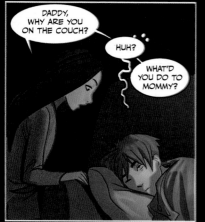

DADDY, WHY ARE YOU ON THE COUCH?

HUH?

WHAT'D YOU DO TO MOMMY?

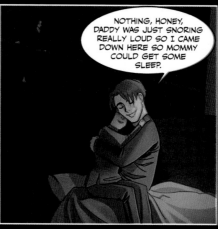

NOTHING, HONEY, DADDY WAS JUST SNORING REALLY LOUD SO I CAME DOWN HERE SO MOMMY COULD GET SOME SLEEP.

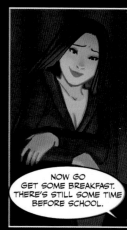

NOW GO GET SOME BREAKFAST. THERE'S STILL SOME TIME BEFORE SCHOOL.

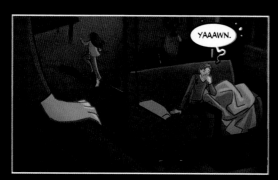

YAAAWN.

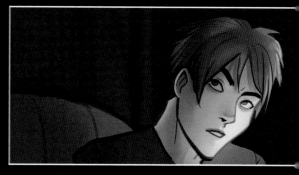

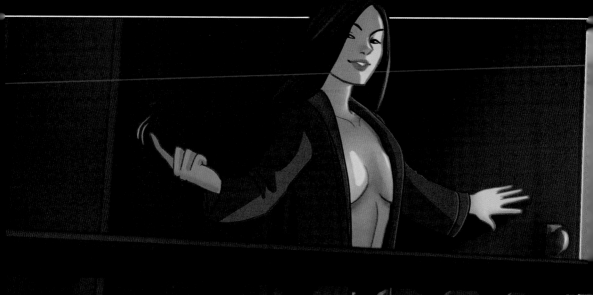

NGGHH...
YOU OKAY?
SWITCH?

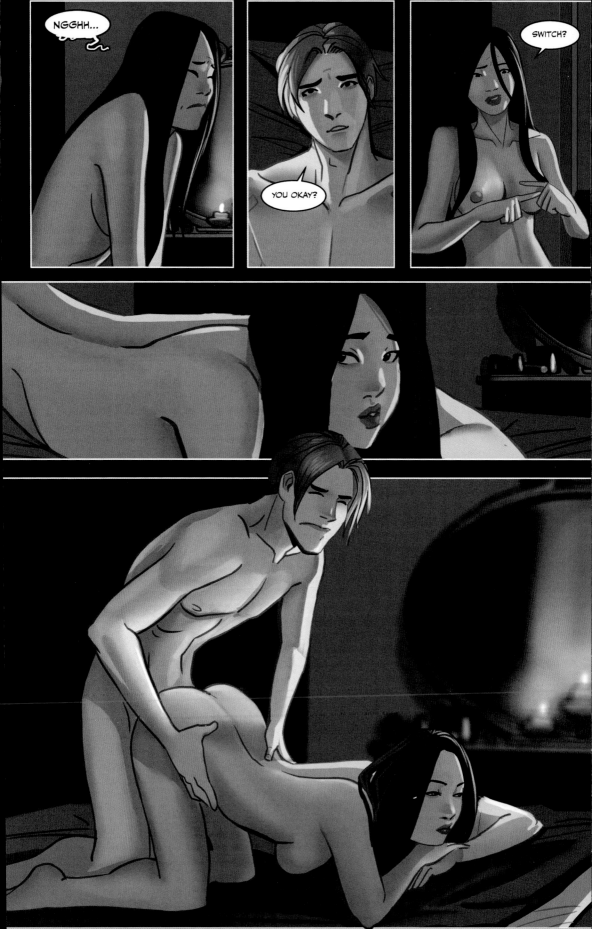

CHAPTER THREE

MY DAYS HAVE BECOME A BLUR OF ROUTINE.

THERE'S NOTHING WRONG WITH MY LIFE.

DADDY, CAN WE HAVE PIZZA TONIGHT?

ALL RIGHT, HAVE A GREAT DAY, KIDS. I'LL PICK YOU UP AFTER SCHOOL.

IT'S GREAT, IN FACT.

PIZZA SOUNDS GOOD. I'LL SEE YOU LATER. LOVE YOU, KIDS!

BYE DADDY!

BUT I STILL FIND MYSELF LONGING FOR SOMETHING MORE.

I WILL WADE OUT
TILL MY THIGHS ARE STEEPED IN BURNING FLOWERS
I WILL TAKE THE SUN IN MY MOUTH
AND LEAP INTO THE RIPE AIR
ALIVE
WITH CLOSED EYES
TO DASH AGAINST DARKNESS

NOT SURE WHY THAT IS.

CAN ANYONE TELL ME WHY E.E. CUMMINGS WROTE THIS WAY?

HE WAS LAZY?

I'M A HIGH SCHOOL ENGLISH TEACHER, AND I'VE GOT THE AMERICAN DREAM.

HOT WIFE. TWO KIDS. HOUSE IN THE SUBURBS. WE'RE ALL HEALTHY.

WRONG!

HE WENT AGAINST ALL THE LAWS OF ENGLISH TO CONVEY HIS MEANINGS WITH A DISREGARD FOR PUNCTUATION AND DECAPITALIZATION.

WHY DO I FEEL A LONGING FOR MORE?

HE CONVEYS LOVE IN A WORD...

SELF-WORTH IN A LETTER...

AND IMAGERY IN A SPACE.

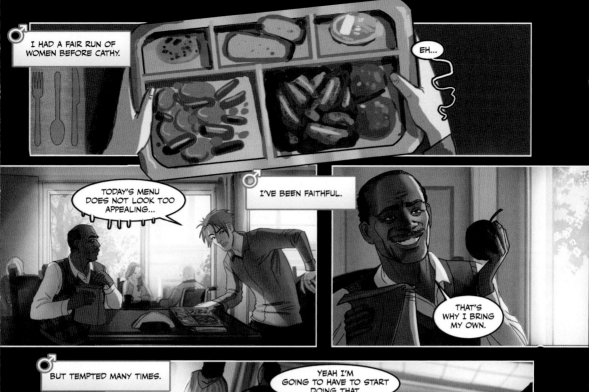

I HAD A FAIR RUN OF WOMEN BEFORE CATHY.

EH...

TODAY'S MENU DOES NOT LOOK TOO APPEALING...

I'VE BEEN FAITHFUL.

THAT'S WHY I BRING MY OWN.

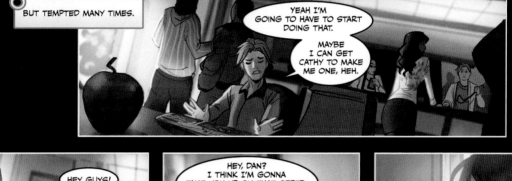

BUT TEMPTED MANY TIMES.

YEAH I'M GOING TO HAVE TO START DOING THAT.

MAYBE I CAN GET CATHY TO MAKE ME ONE, HEH.

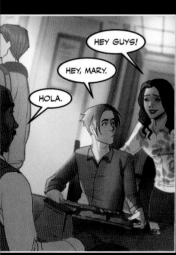

HEY GUYS!

HEY, MARY.

HOLA.

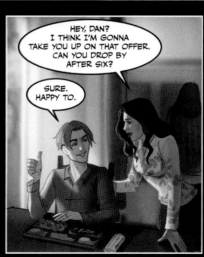

HEY, DAN? I THINK I'M GONNA TAKE YOU UP ON THAT OFFER. CAN YOU DROP BY AFTER SIX?

SURE. HAPPY TO.

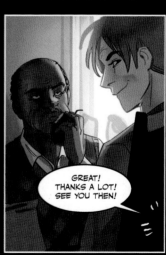

GREAT! THANKS A LOT! SEE YOU THEN!

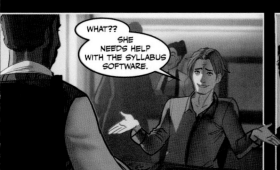

WHAT??

SHE NEEDS HELP WITH THE SYLLABUS SOFTWARE.

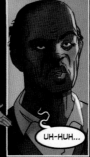

UH-HUH...

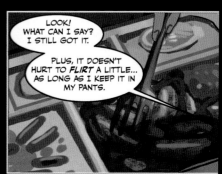

LOOK! WHAT CAN I SAY? I STILL GOT IT.

PLUS, IT DOESN'T HURT TO FLIRT A LITTLE... AS LONG AS I KEEP IT IN MY PANTS.

MY DAYS HAVE BECOME A BLUR OF ROUTINE.
THIS IS WHAT WE HAVE.
I WORK FOR A COMPANY THAT MAKES TRAILERS FOR MOVIES AND THE AFFILIATED MARKETING WEBSITES.
THE WHOLE TEAM WAS UP ALL NIGHT, BUT WE WON'T HAVE THE TRAILER DONE UNTIL TOMORROW.
YEAH... NO WAY.
ALL RIGHT GUYS, I'M HAVING LUNCH WITH THE CLIENT SO I'LL BUY US MORE TIME.
EMAIL ME A LINK OF WHAT WE HAVE.
WORLD TOLD ME I COULD HAVE IT ALL.
CAREER.
POSTAL
LOVE.
FAMILY.
MOM WANTED ME TO BE A HOUSEWIFE...
MOM
STILL DOES.

BUT WHAT DID THAT EVER GET HER?
<HI MOM.>
AFTER I HAD ASHLEY, MY DAD LEFT HER AND MARRIED A YOUNGER WOMAN WHO GAVE HIM MORE CHILDREN.
<I CAN'T DO THAT, MOM.>
<DAN PICKS THE KIDS UP FROM SCHOOL. I DON'T GET HOME UNTIL AFTER EIGHT MOST NIGHTS, DEPENDING ON TRAFFIC.>
NOW SHE CALLS ME EVERY DAY TO TELL ME HOW TO LIVE MY LIFE, SINCE SHE DOESN'T HAVE ONE OF HER OWN.
<I KNOW. OKAY. I LOVE YOU TOO.>
SIGH...
I'M SUPPORTING HER FINANCIALLY, SO YOU'D THINK THAT WOULD GIVE ME A PASS.
I'M HER ONLY CHILD AND SHE MEANS WELL, BUT IT GETS TIRING.

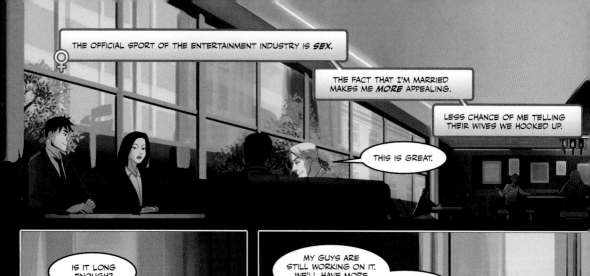

THE OFFICIAL SPORT OF THE ENTERTAINMENT INDUSTRY IS *SEX.*

THE FACT THAT I'M MARRIED MAKES ME *MORE* APPEALING.

LESS CHANCE OF ME TELLING THEIR WIVES WE HOOKED UP.

THIS IS GREAT.

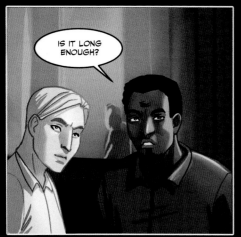

IS IT LONG ENOUGH?

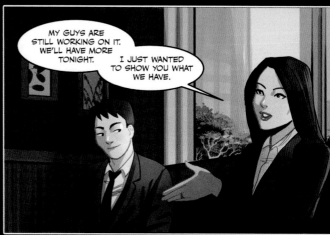

MY GUYS ARE STILL WORKING ON IT. WE'LL HAVE MORE TONIGHT.

I JUST WANTED TO SHOW YOU WHAT WE HAVE.

7 p.m.

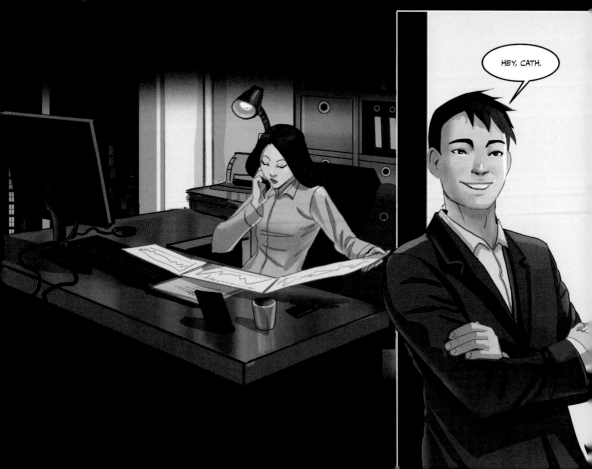

HEY, CATH.

I'VE NEVER CHEATED, THOUGH.
I SPOKE TO THE CLIENT. THOSE GUYS LOVE YOU.
POSTAL
Pure Chemistry
YEAH. IT SEEMED TO GO WELL.
BUT SOMETIMES IT'S VERY TEMPTING...
TERRIFIC WORK, AS ALWAYS. THIS PLACE WOULD FALL APART WITHOUT YOU.
CAN I BUY YOU A DRINK... TO CELEBRATE?
NO --
NO THANKS.
I'VE GOT TO GET HOME AND HELP THE KIDS WITH THEIR HOMEWORK.
BUT THANKS, CHRIS, YOU'RE THE BEST ASSISTANT I'VE EVER HAD.
LIFE IS SHORT!
CHEAT ON IT!
www.washley-adison.com
I COULD GET AWAY WITH IT.
NO ONE WOULD KNOW.
-- I WOULD... *SIGH.*

OKAY, I THINK IT'S READY.
DON'T MESS IT UP.
SHUT UP!!! DAD, PLEASE TELL BLAKE TO SHUT UP!
SHHH...
MOM!
YOU'RE JUST IN TIME.
FOR WHAT?
ASHLEY'S GOING TO BLOW UP THE KITCHEN!
SHUT UP!!
HUSH, LITTLE MAN.
LET'S WATCH YOUR SISTER DO SOME MAD SCIENCE.
GLUG GLUG GLUG

IT WORKED!
MAYBE MOM IS RIGHT.
GOOD JOB, HONEY.
YOU'RE GOING TO KNOCK 'EM DEAD TOMORROW AT THE SCIENCE FAIR.
THEY'RE ONLY GOING TO BE YOUNG LIKE THIS ONCE.
SORRY I'M LATE. 405 TRAFFIC WAS SO BAD TONIGHT.
I MISS SO MUCH BEING GONE 12 HOURS A DAY.
I'M SO HUNGRY! WHAT'D YOU GUYS DO FOR DINNER?
DAN IS A GOOD MAN. HE'S GOOD WITH THE KIDS.
WE SAVED SOME FOR YOU...WHICH WAS HARD WITH THESE LITTLE HOOVERS WE HAVE TO FEED.
THEY'RE REALLY STARTING TO EAT A LOT.
I LEARNED A LONG TIME AGO THAT CATHY NEEDS ME TO LISTEN TO HER FOR *15 MINUTES* EVERY NIGHT.
SHE NEVER WANTS MY OPINION ON THINGS -- SHE JUST WANTS TO VENT.
LEARNED THAT THE HARD WAY, BUT NOW I ASK AND LISTEN.
SO, HOW WAS WORK TODAY?
I HAD LUNCH WITH THE CLIENT TODAY.
WHAT IS IT WITH GAY GUYS IN LA BEING SO BUFF

6:00 a.m.

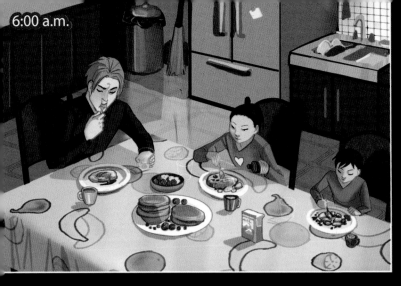

6:00 a.m.

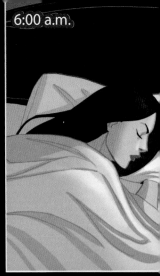

5:00 p.m.

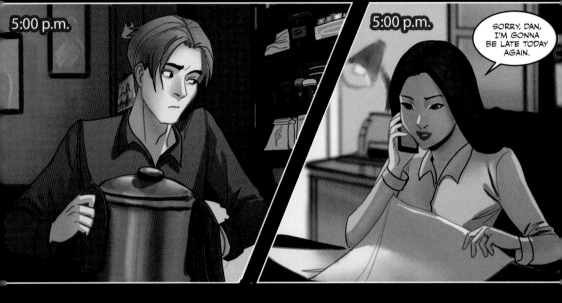

SORRY, DAN, I'M GONNA BE LATE TODAY AGAIN.

9:00 p.m.

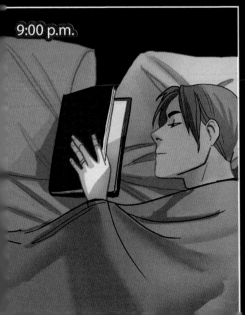

9:00 p.m.

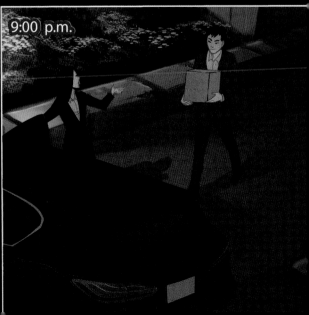

8:30 a.m.

8:30 a.m.

:00 p.m.

6:00 p.m.

:00 p.m.

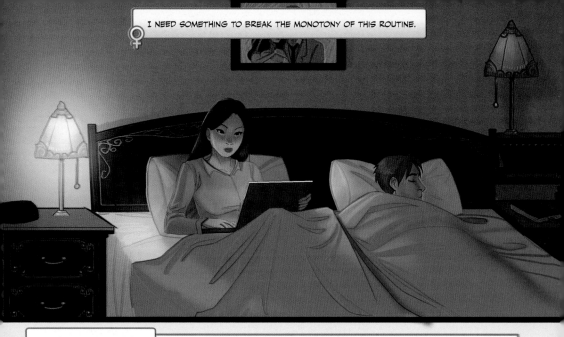

I NEED SOMETHING TO BREAK THE MONOTONY OF THIS ROUTINE.

SOMETHING EXCITING.

Goodle How to spice up a marriage

About 6,234,890 results, 0.001 seconds

10 Kinky Ways to Spice up Sex Life
www.establishyoursexlifeword.com

Blah blah blablalah meh blele brblle blah blablabla.
bla. Blah blabla meh blah meh meh. Blah blah blablalah meh blele brblle blah blablabla.
meh blele brblle blah blablabla bla. Blah blabla meh blah meh meh.

Improve Your Relationship- Spice Up Your Marriage
www.usefulrelationshipadvicemagazine.com

Blah blah blablalah meh blele brblle blah blablabla. Blah blah blablalah meh blele brblle blah blablabla.
bla. Blah blabla meh blah meh meh. Blah blah blablalah meh blah meh meh.
blele brblle blah blablabla blele brblle blah blablabla.

Save Your Marriage- Blow in His Ear
www.blowinginhisearsaveyourmarriage.com

blele brblle blah blablabla blele brblle blah blablabla blele brblle blah blablabla.
blele brblle blah blablabla blele brblle blah blablabla.

Spice Up Your Relationship by Swinging
www.swingers.com

Blah blah blablalah meh blele brblle blah blablabla.
bla. Blah blabla meh blah meh meh. Blah blah blablalah meh blele brblle blah blablabla.
eh blablabla brblle blah blablabla. Blah blabla meh blah meh meh. Blah blah blablalah meh blele brblle blah blablabla.
Blah blah blablalah meh blele brblle blah blablabla blele brblle blah blablabla bla. Blah blabla meh blah meh meh.
bla. Blah blabla meh blah meh meh.

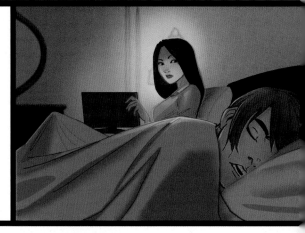

Spice Up Your Relationship by Swinging
www.swingers.com

HMMM...
SNOOREEE
BWAH!!
OH! SO YOU'RE AWAKE?
UH...YEAH!

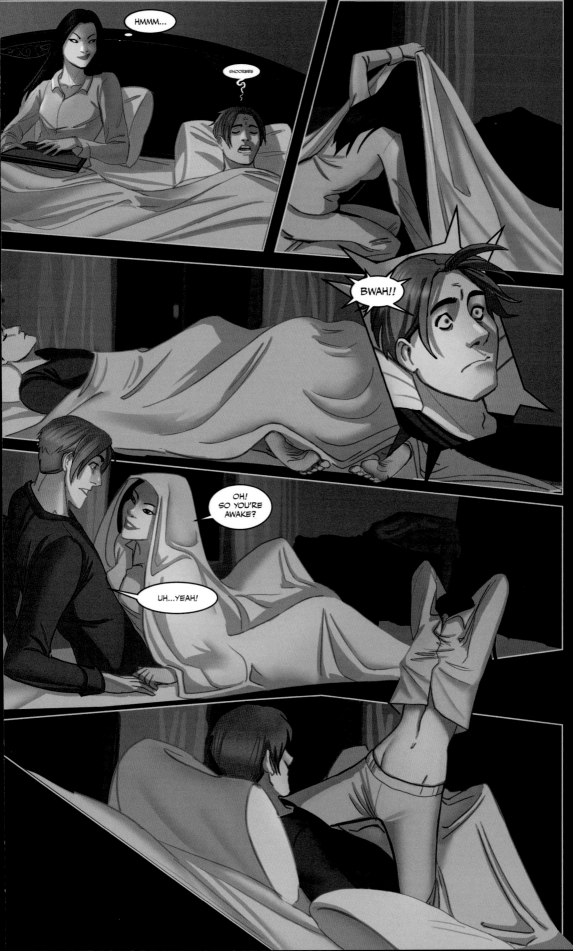

SNOREEEE
CATHY.
SNOREEE!
CATHY?
M-MMM...
FLIP
SHAKE
SHAKE
CATHY
YOU HAVE TO GET UP OR
YOU'RE GOING TO BE LATE
FOR WORK.
AAH!!
I'M UP!

YOU WERE WILD LAST NIGHT.
CAN'T THINK OF THE LAST TIME YOU WOKE ME UP FOR SEX.
I WAS READING ABOUT SWINGER SITES.
I THINK I'D LIKE TO TRY THAT.
WHAT?

I WOULD REALLY LIKE TO HAVE SEX WITH OTHER WOMEN...
DO'S AND DON'TS OF SWINGING
BE HONEST ABOUT YOUR BOUNDARIES
ARGUE IN PUBLIC
BE DISCRETE
...BUT AM I GOING TO BE OKAY WATCHING ANOTHER GUY HAVE SEX WITH CATH?
WHAT IF THE GUY IS BETTER THAN ME?
WHAT IF HIS DICK IS BIGGER THAN MINE?
WHAT IF THE SEX IS SO GOOD FOR HER THAT SHE LEAVES ME FOR HIM?
WHAT IF I DISAPPOINT THE GIRL I'M WITH?
WHAT IF SOME GUY STARTS STALKING CATHY?
I'M DONE, MR. LINCOLN.
SLAM

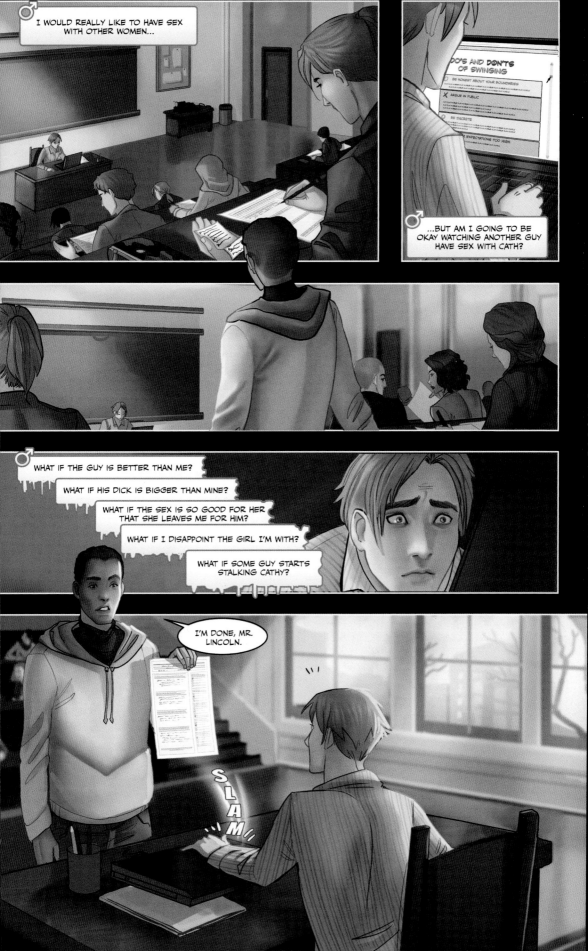

IT'S SO GREAT TO SEE YOU AGAIN, DEBBIE!
I MISS OUR CRAZY COLLEGE DAYS TOGETHER. I THINK ABOUT THEM ALL THE TIME...
ARE YOU STILL DATING JOEL?
OH GOD NO...
HEH... HE WAS LIKE FOUR GUYS AGO.
I'M A BIT JEALOUS OF YOUR BEING SINGLE AND ABLE TO DATE.
I'VE NEVER EVEN HAD ONE OF THOSE ONLINE DATING PROFILES.
I FEEL LIKE I'VE MISSED OUT.
GRASS IS ALWAYS GREENER AS THEY SAY.
I ENVY YOU YOUR STABILITY AND AMAZING LIFE.
DAN'S A GOOD GUY, THERE ARE A LOT OF ASSHOLES OUT THERE.
I GET THAT, BUT SERIOUSLY...YOU REALIZE I'VE ONLY ***EVER*** HAD SEX WITH DAN.
WHAT IF YOU MARRIED YOUR FIRST?
MARK? OMG, HE'S FAT AND BALD NOW. I'D KILL MYSELF.
OUT OF CURIOSITY... HOW MANY MEN ***HAVE*** YOU SLEPT WITH?
HMM. LEMME THINK...
I DUNNO...
FORTY?
FIFTY?
WHO COUNTS AT THIS POINT?

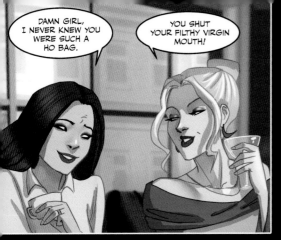

DAMN GIRL, I NEVER KNEW YOU WERE SUCH A HO BAG.

YOU SHUT YOUR FILTHY VIRGIN MOUTH!

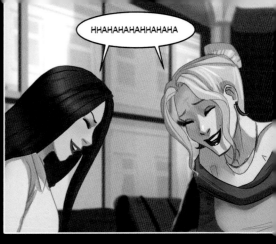

HHAHAHAHAHHAHAHA

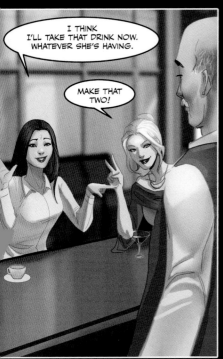

I THINK I'LL TAKE THAT DRINK NOW. WHATEVER SHE'S HAVING.

MAKE THAT TWO!

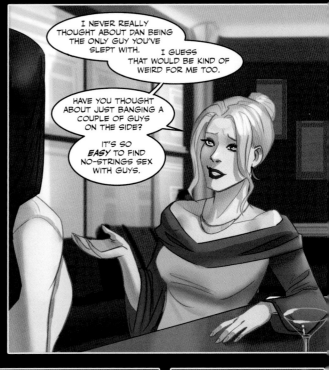

I NEVER REALLY THOUGHT ABOUT DAN BEING THE ONLY GUY YOU'VE SLEPT WITH. I GUESS THAT WOULD BE KIND OF WEIRD FOR ME TOO.

HAVE YOU THOUGHT ABOUT JUST BANGING A COUPLE OF GUYS ON THE SIDE?

IT'S SO *EASY* TO FIND NO-STRINGS SEX WITH GUYS.

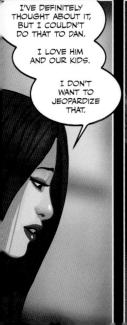

I'VE DEFINITELY THOUGHT ABOUT IT, BUT I COULDN'T DO THAT TO DAN.

I LOVE HIM AND OUR KIDS.

I DON'T WANT TO JEOPARDIZE THAT.

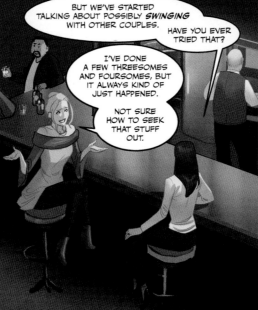

BUT WE'VE STARTED TALKING ABOUT POSSIBLY *SWINGING* WITH OTHER COUPLES. HAVE YOU EVER TRIED THAT?

I'VE DONE A FEW THREESOMES AND FOURSOMES, BUT IT ALWAYS KIND OF JUST HAPPENED.

NOT SURE HOW TO SEEK THAT STUFF OUT.

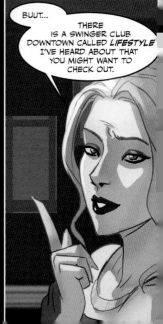

BUUT... THERE IS A SWINGER CLUB DOWNTOWN CALLED *LIFESTYLE* I'VE HEARD ABOUT THAT YOU MIGHT WANT TO CHECK OUT.

HAVE YOU EVER BEEN WITH ANOTHER GIRL?
MOST OF THE SWINGER WOMEN I'VE MET ARE *BISEXUAL*.
I'M NOT OPPOSED TO IT, BUT NO I'VE NOT BEEN WITH A WOMAN.
I'M NOT SURE HOW I FEEL ABOUT THAT, ACTUALLY.
WELL, DISCOVERING WHAT YOU LIKE IS PART OF THE FUN I GUESS.
YOU SURE YOU'RE OK WATCHING DAN FUCK ANOTHER GIRL?
WHAT IF SHE'S HOTTER THAN YOU?
YEAH...
WHAT IF SHE IS HOTTER THAN ME?
WHAT IF SHE GIVES A BETTER BJ THAN I DO?
WHAT IF HE STARTS SEEING HER ON THE SIDE?
WHAT IF THE KIDS OR MY MOM FIND OUT?

CHAPTER FOUR

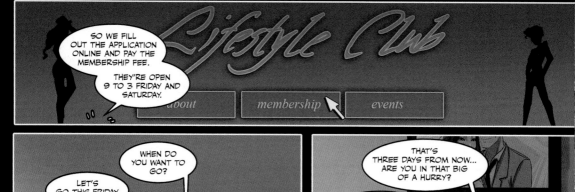

SO WE FILL OUT THE APPLICATION ONLINE AND PAY THE MEMBERSHIP FEE.

THEY'RE OPEN 9 TO 3 FRIDAY AND SATURDAY.

Lifestyle Club

about | membership | events

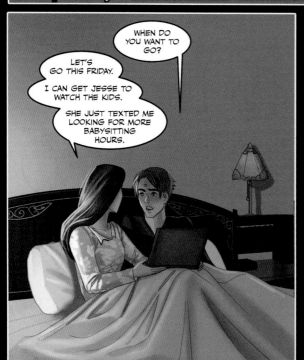

WHEN DO YOU WANT TO GO?

LET'S GO THIS FRIDAY.

I CAN GET JESSE TO WATCH THE KIDS.

SHE JUST TEXTED ME LOOKING FOR MORE BABYSITTING HOURS.

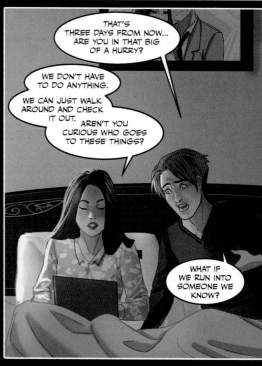

THAT'S THREE DAYS FROM NOW... ARE YOU IN THAT BIG OF A HURRY?

WE DON'T HAVE TO DO ANYTHING.

WE CAN JUST WALK AROUND AND CHECK IT OUT.

AREN'T YOU CURIOUS WHO GOES TO THESE THINGS?

WHAT IF WE RUN INTO SOMEONE WE KNOW?

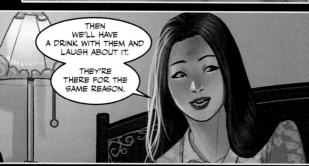

THEN WE'LL HAVE A DRINK WITH THEM AND LAUGH ABOUT IT.

THEY'RE THERE FOR THE SAME REASON.

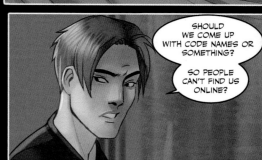

SHOULD WE COME UP WITH CODE NAMES OR SOMETHING?

SO PEOPLE CAN'T FIND US ONLINE?

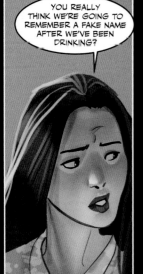

YOU REALLY THINK WE'RE GOING TO REMEMBER A FAKE NAME AFTER WE'VE BEEN DRINKING?

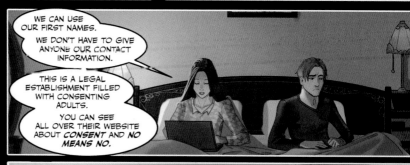

WE CAN USE OUR FIRST NAMES.

WE DON'T HAVE TO GIVE ANYONE OUR CONTACT INFORMATION.

THIS IS A LEGAL ESTABLISHMENT FILLED WITH CONSENTING ADULTS.

YOU CAN SEE ALL OVER THEIR WEBSITE ABOUT *CONSENT* AND *NO MEANS NO*.

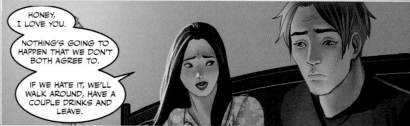

HONEY, I LOVE YOU.

NOTHING'S GOING TO HAPPEN THAT WE DON'T BOTH AGREE TO.

IF WE HATE IT, WE'LL WALK AROUND, HAVE A COUPLE DRINKS AND LEAVE.

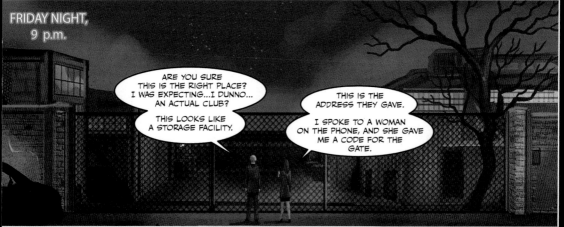

FRIDAY NIGHT, 9 p.m.

ARE YOU SURE THIS IS THE RIGHT PLACE? I WAS EXPECTING...I DUNNO... AN ACTUAL CLUB?

THIS LOOKS LIKE A STORAGE FACILITY.

THIS IS THE ADDRESS THEY GAVE.

I SPOKE TO A WOMAN ON THE PHONE, AND SHE GAVE ME A CODE FOR THE GATE.

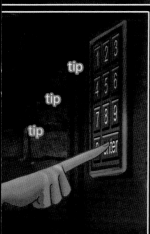

tip
tip
tip

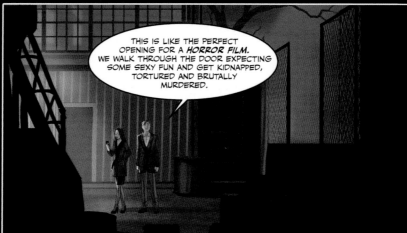

THIS IS LIKE THE PERFECT OPENING FOR A *HORROR FILM.* WE WALK THROUGH THE DOOR EXPECTING SOME SEXY FUN AND GET KIDNAPPED, TORTURED AND BRUTALLY MURDERED.

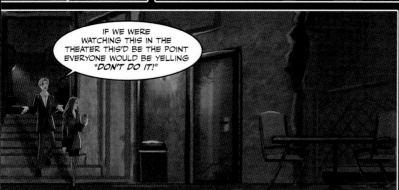

IF WE WERE WATCHING THIS IN THE THEATER THIS'D BE THE POINT EVERYONE WOULD BE YELLING *"DON'T DO IT!"*

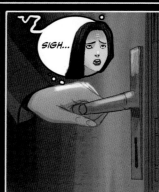

SIGH...

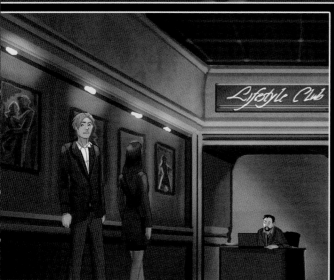

Lifestyle Club

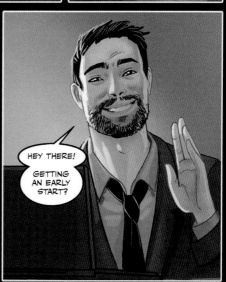

HEY THERE!

GETTING AN EARLY START?

WHAT DO YOU MEAN?
WE OPEN AT 9, BUT THE PLACE DOESN'T REALLY START HOPPING FOR A WHILE.
CAN I SEE YOUR IDS?
FIRST TIME HERE?
YEAH. IS IT THAT OBVIOUS?
CALIFORNIA
I JUST DON'T RECOGNIZE YOU... WOULD YOU LIKE A TOUR?
MY NAME'S CARL, MY WIFE AND I OWN THE PLACE.
SURE!
THAT WOULD BE GREAT, THANKS.
SHEILA!
SIGH...CARL...
I BOUGHT THESE FOR A REASON!
YOU KNOW I HATE IT WHEN YOU'RE YELLING AT ME LIKE SOME DOG TO ITS MASTER.
UH, SORRY HON, CAN YOU GIVE THIS COUPLE A TOUR?
SURE, ARE WE OPEN?
THE BARTENDER GIRLS AREN'T EVEN HERE YET.

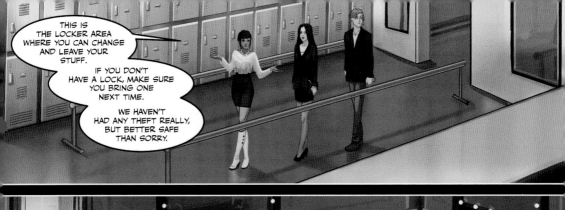

THIS IS THE LOCKER AREA WHERE YOU CAN CHANGE AND LEAVE YOUR STUFF.

IF YOU DON'T HAVE A LOCK, MAKE SURE YOU BRING ONE NEXT TIME.

WE HAVEN'T HAD ANY THEFT REALLY, BUT BETTER SAFE THAN SORRY.

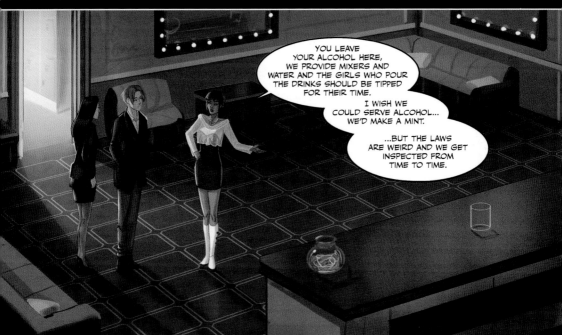

YOU LEAVE YOUR ALCOHOL HERE, WE PROVIDE MIXERS AND WATER AND THE GIRLS WHO POUR THE DRINKS SHOULD BE TIPPED FOR THEIR TIME.

I WISH WE COULD SERVE ALCOHOL... WE'D MAKE A MINT.

...BUT THE LAWS ARE WEIRD AND WE GET INSPECTED FROM TIME TO TIME.

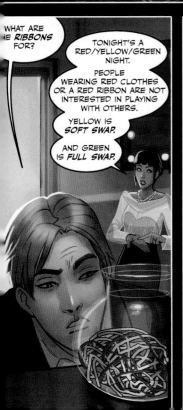

WHAT ARE THE RIBBONS FOR?

TONIGHT'S A RED/YELLOW/GREEN NIGHT.

PEOPLE WEARING RED CLOTHES OR A RED RIBBON ARE NOT INTERESTED IN PLAYING WITH OTHERS.

YELLOW IS SOFT SWAP.

AND GREEN IS FULL SWAP.

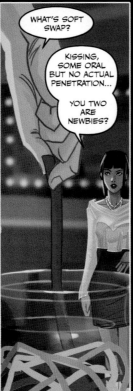

WHAT'S SOFT SWAP?

KISSING, SOME ORAL BUT NO ACTUAL PENETRATION...

YOU TWO ARE NEWBIES?

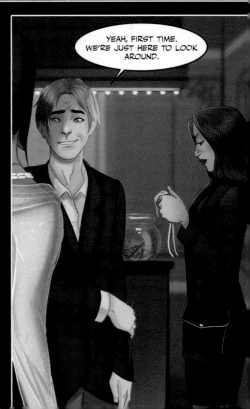

YEAH, FIRST TIME. WE'RE JUST HERE TO LOOK AROUND.

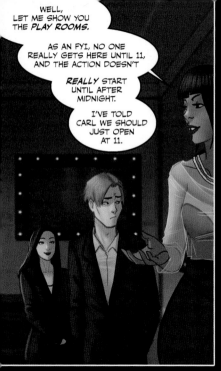

WELL, LET ME SHOW YOU THE *PLAY ROOMS*.

AS AN FYI, NO ONE REALLY GETS HERE UNTIL 11, AND THE ACTION DOESN'T

REALLY START UNTIL AFTER MIDNIGHT.

I'VE TOLD CARL WE SHOULD JUST OPEN AT 11.

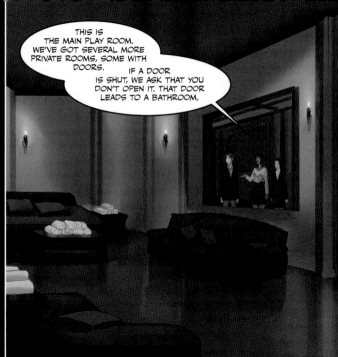

THIS IS THE MAIN PLAY ROOM. WE'VE GOT SEVERAL MORE PRIVATE ROOMS, SOME WITH DOORS.

IF A DOOR IS SHUT, WE ASK THAT YOU DON'T OPEN IT. THAT DOOR LEADS TO A BATHROOM.

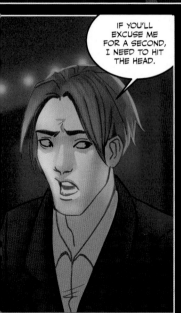

IF YOU'LL EXCUSE ME FOR A SECOND, I NEED TO HIT THE HEAD.

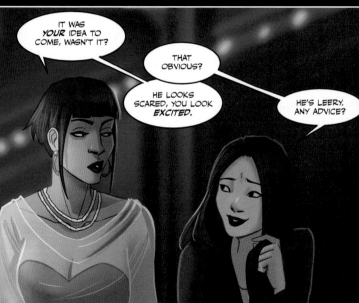

IT WAS *YOUR* IDEA TO COME, WASN'T IT?

THAT OBVIOUS?

HE LOOKS SCARED, YOU LOOK *EXCITED*.

HE'S LEERY. ANY ADVICE?

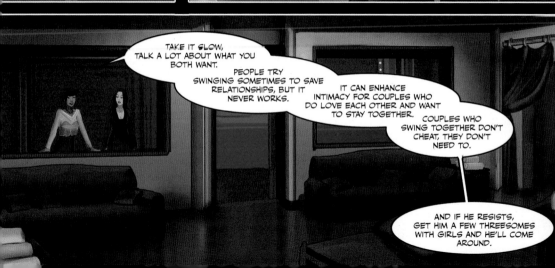

TAKE IT SLOW, TALK A LOT ABOUT WHAT YOU BOTH WANT.

PEOPLE TRY SWINGING SOMETIMES TO SAVE RELATIONSHIPS, BUT IT NEVER WORKS.

IT CAN ENHANCE INTIMACY FOR COUPLES WHO DO LOVE EACH OTHER AND WANT TO STAY TOGETHER.

COUPLES WHO SWING TOGETHER DON'T CHEAT, THEY DON'T NEED TO.

AND IF HE RESISTS, GET HIM A FEW THREESOMES WITH GIRLS AND HE'LL COME AROUND.

DO YOU KNOW WHAT TIME IT IS?
NOPE, PHONE'S IN THE LOCKER.
IT'S ELEVEN.
I'VE GOT TO STOP DRINKING SO I CAN DRIVE.
WHAT TIME DO WE HAVE TO BE HOME FOR THE BABYSITTER?
MIDNIGHT...
SHIT... LET ME GO GET MY PHONE AND CALL HER TO SEE IF SHE CAN STAY A BIT LATER.
YOU WANT TO *STAY?*
YOU'VE HAD WHAT, FOUR DRINKS? YOU CAN'T DRIVE FOR ANOTHER HOUR, HOUR AND A HALF AT LEAST...
PLUS WE HAVEN'T EVEN SEEN ANYTHING YET. NO ONE'S GONE BACK TO THE PLAYROOMS.
YAWN.
LET'S JUST GO, I'LL GET US AN UBER AND COME GET THE CAR TOMORROW.
I'M *NOT* LEAVING MY CAR HERE.
I'LL GO CALL HER, IT'LL BE FINE.
I'LL TAKE YOU IN THE BACK AND SUCK YOUR COCK WHEN I GET BACK.
SHE'S A *KEEPER.*

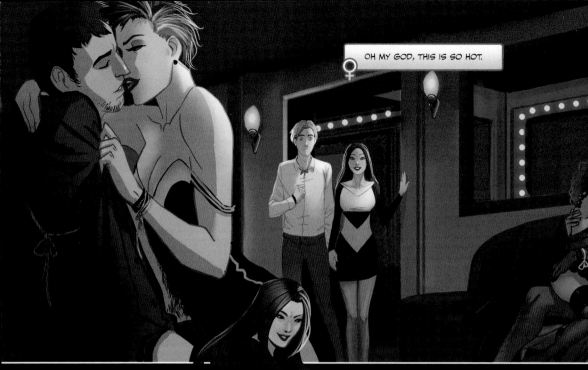

OH MY GOD, THIS IS SO HOT.

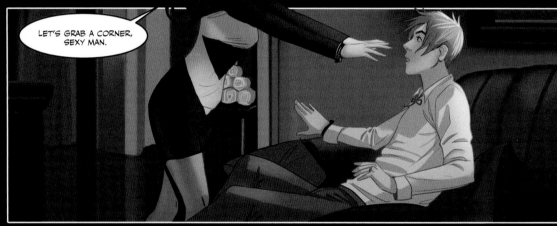

LET'S GRAB A CORNER, SEXY MAN.

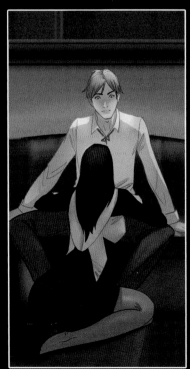
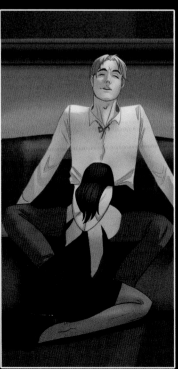
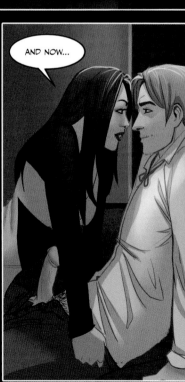

AND NOW...

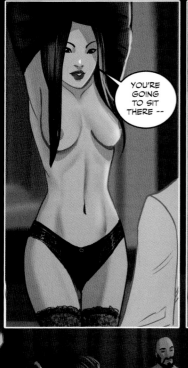

YOU'RE GOING TO SIT THERE --

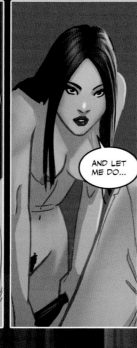

AND LET ME DO...

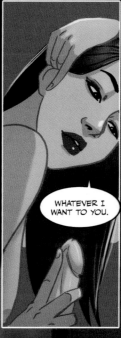

WHATEVER I WANT TO YOU.

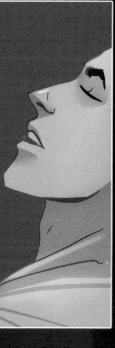

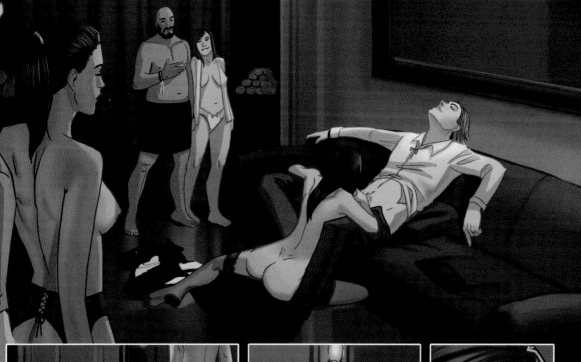

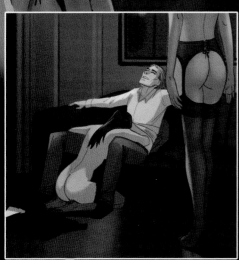

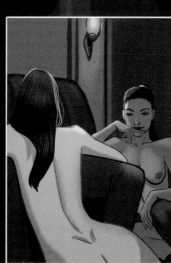

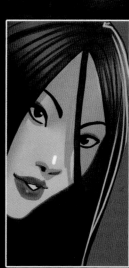

WHAT THE FUCK?

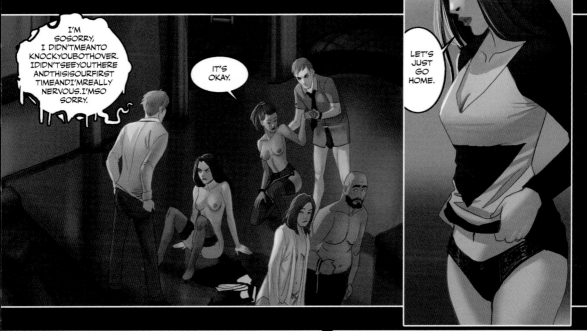

I'M SOSORRY, I DIDN'TMEANTO KNOCKYOUBOTHOVER. IDIDN'TSEEYOUTHERE ANDTHISISOURFIRST TIMEANDI'MREALLY NERVOUS.I'MSO SORRY.

IT'S OKAY.

LET'S JUST GO HOME.

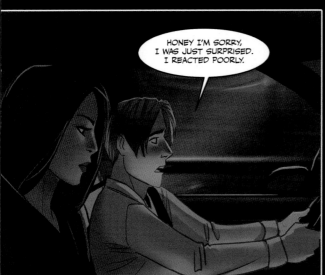

HONEY I'M SORRY, I WAS JUST SURPRISED. I REACTED POORLY.

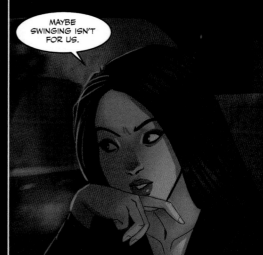

MAYBE SWINGING ISN'T FOR US.

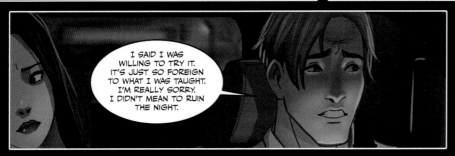

I SAID I WAS WILLING TO TRY IT. IT'S JUST SO FOREIGN TO WHAT I WAS TAUGHT. I'M REALLY SORRY. I DIDN'T MEAN TO RUIN THE NIGHT.

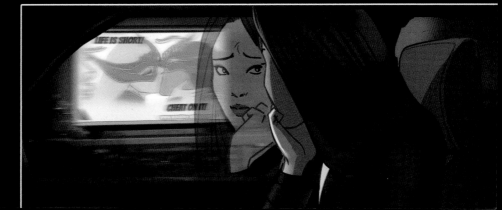

LIFE IS SHORT!

CHEAT ON IT!

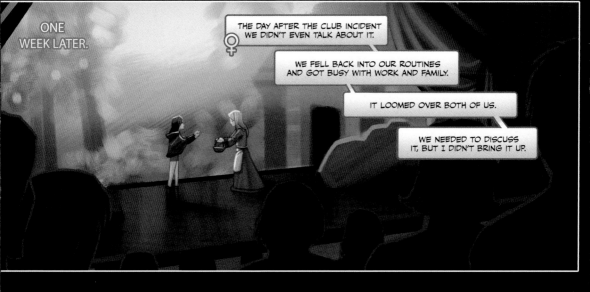

ONE WEEK LATER.

THE DAY AFTER THE CLUB INCIDENT WE DIDN'T EVEN TALK ABOUT IT.

WE FELL BACK INTO OUR ROUTINES AND GOT BUSY WITH WORK AND FAMILY.

IT LOOMED OVER BOTH OF US.

WE NEEDED TO DISCUSS IT, BUT I DIDN'T BRING IT UP.

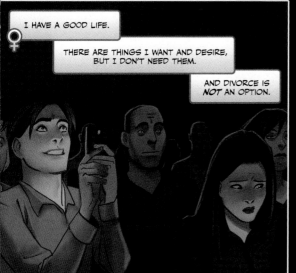

I HAVE A GOOD LIFE.

THERE ARE THINGS I WANT AND DESIRE, BUT I DON'T NEED THEM.

AND DIVORCE IS *NOT* AN OPTION.

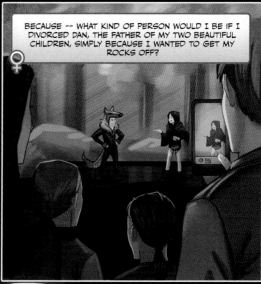

BECAUSE -- WHAT KIND OF PERSON WOULD I BE IF I DIVORCED DAN, THE FATHER OF MY TWO BEAUTIFUL CHILDREN, SIMPLY BECAUSE I WANTED TO GET MY ROCKS OFF?

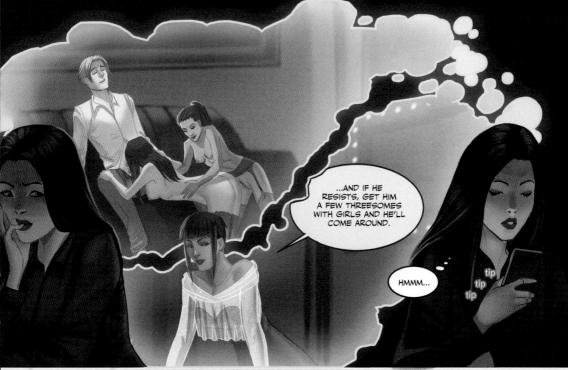

...AND IF HE RESISTS, GET HIM A FEW THREESOMES WITH GIRLS AND HE'LL COME AROUND.

HMMM...

tip
tip
tip

WOULD YOU DO A THREEWAY WITH DAN AND I?
ASHLEY FLUBBED HER LINE.
HUH?
OH...
PLEASE DON'T SAY ANYTHING TO HER.
PLINK
ARE YOU SERIOUS?
YEAH.
OUR FIRST ATTEMPT AT A SEX CLUB WAS A BUST.
A WOMAN THERE TOLD ME THAT THE BEST WAY TO GET A GUY COMFORTABLE WITH THE LIFESTYLE IS TO GET HIM THREESOMES.
YEAH I'D DO IT FOR YOU HON
WHEN DO YOU WANT TO DO IT?
WHAT ARE THE RULES?
TIP TIP TIP
TIP TIP TIP
YOU FREE TONIGHT?
WE CAN WORK OUT DETAILS IN PERSON.
LOL OKAY WHAT TIME?
LET'S DROP ASHLEY OFF AT MY MOM'S, BLAKE'S ALREADY THERE.
SHE WON'T MIND, SHE LOVES THE KIDS.
WE COULD USE SOME ALONE TIME.
SOUNDS GOOD, BABY.

THANK GOD CATHY'S NOT STILL UPSET WITH ME.
I'VE BEEN WANTING TO TALK TO HER ABOUT IT, BUT WASN'T SURE HOW TO START IT.
I'LL GO DOWN ON HER UNTIL SHE CAN'T TAKE ANY MORE.
AFTER WE'RE DONE, WE CAN TALK ABOUT THAT.
IT'S JUST THE THREE OF US.

THOUGH...
YOU'LL HAVE TO USE A CONDOM TODAY.
OH -- KAY!
I MEAN... IF THIS IS OKAY WITH YOU...
UH... BOTH OF YOU.
OH, RELAX, DAN. IN A WAY IT'S LIKE THAT TIME WE HAD A FONDUE PARTY!
A BUNCH OF FRIENDS TOGETHER, DIPPING STUFF!
WHAT? BAD ICEBREAKER?
AH, FUCK IT! I TRIED THE NICE WAY!
NOW WE DO IT MY WAY.
HEY!
GET IN THERE, CATHY!
AND I'LL JUST ROLL WITH THE FONDUE PARTY METAPHOR.

AND DIP IN!
OH...MMM... OKAY...I MEAN... MMM FEEL FREE TO DOUBLE DIP!
CATHY, SCOOT OVER!
REMEMBER THE FIRST RULE OF A THREESOME: SHARING IS CARING!
OH, SO NOW YOU KNOW THE RULES?
OH YEAH!
I'LL FILL YOU IN AS WE GO.

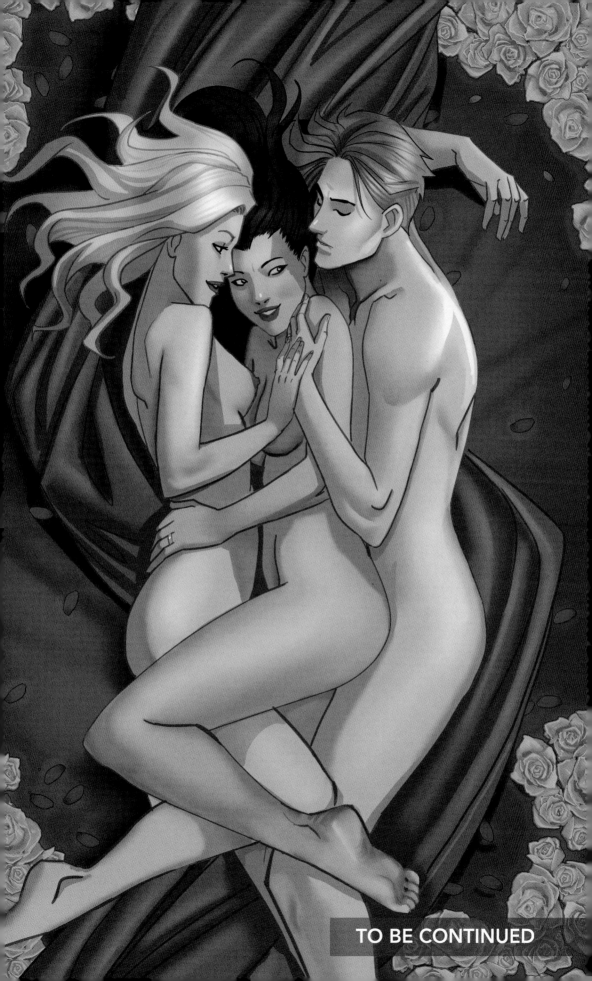

TO BE CONTINUED

SW

VOLUME

20

JENNI CHEUNG

MATT HAWKINS

NG

TWO

19

LINDA SEJIC

YISHAN LI

JENNI CHEUNG & MATT HAWKINS

The wife/husband writing team live an interesting life together. How much is autobiographical and how much is fiction? She's a web developer by day, he's a comic book nerd that also writes other titles like POSTAL, THINK TANK, SYMMETRY, APHRODITE IX and CYBER FORCE.

LINDA SEJIC

Linda is a digital comics artist specializing in an expressive, dynamic, art style. Her first major project with Top Cow was WILDFIRE, written by Matt Hawkins, which showcased her unconventional, character-focused technique and established her as an up-and-coming talent. Her critically acclaimed webcomic BLOOD STAIN is currently published in print from Top Cow, and is on its third volume. Linda lives in Croatia with her husband, illustrator Stjepan Sejic.

Blood Stain
LOOK!

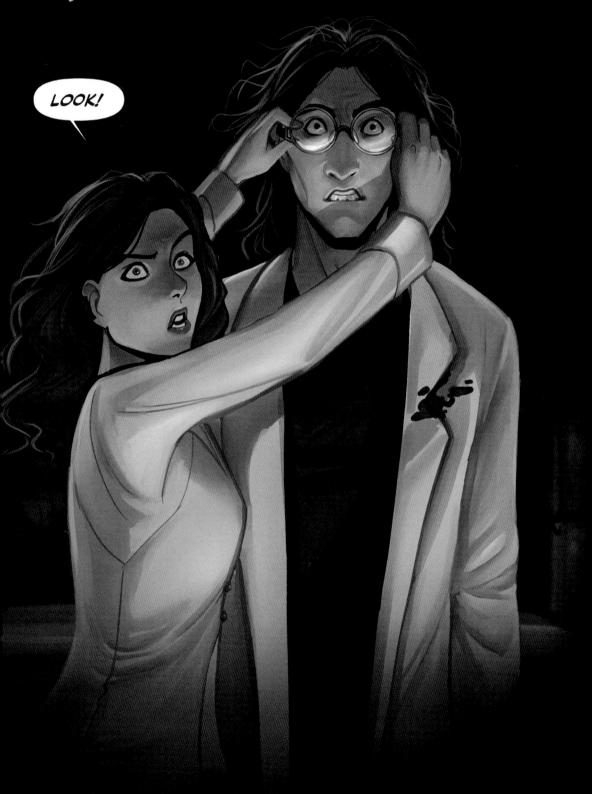

TLACK
TLACK!
CREEAK
GOD... WHAT IS THAT AWFUL SMELL?
LIKE SOMETHING ROTTEN...
WORST CASE
OH NO.
SCENARIO

NO...
NO. NO.
NO NO NO.
OH, GOD...
PLEASE.
TLACK!
TLACK!
PLEASE DON'T BE DEAD, BOSS...
I ONLY JUST GOT HERE...
tlack
tlack
WHAT DO I DO..?
CHECK HIS PULSE?

SNORE!!!
EEP!!
MRNFFF
SNOOORE
OH *THANK GOD...*
HE IS ASLEEP...
I DON'T HAVE TO LOOK FOR ANOTHER JOB...
HMM.
WAS HE HERE ALL NIGHT?
HE LOOKS EXHAUSTED...
I BETTER NOT WAKE HIM...

TIP
TIP
TIP
TIP
TIP
TIP
PHEW... I GUESS I'M DONE FOR NOW... I'LL USE THE AUTOCLAVE LATER, WHEN HE WAKES UP.

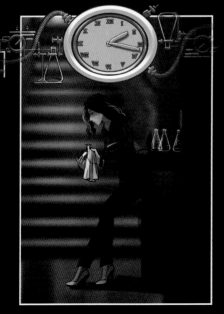

HUH?
OH... HI, SERGE.
HI.
DUDE!!!
ARE YOU STILL ASLEEP??
UMN...
HEY!!
WAKE UP!
UGH...WHAT?
DON'T YOU HAVE CLASSES TODAY!?

CRICK
OH...
RIGHT...
WHAT TIME IS IT?
2:20.
SHIT!!!
OH...
OH-OH.
OH, NO...
WHERE ARE THEY??
KRRR..
TESTS
TESTS
TESTS...
KRRR
WHERE DID I PUT THEM...

MUMBLE MUMBLE MUMBLE MUMBLE MUMBLE
ARRGH...
NO.
NO...
AH!
YES!
PHEW...
OKAY.

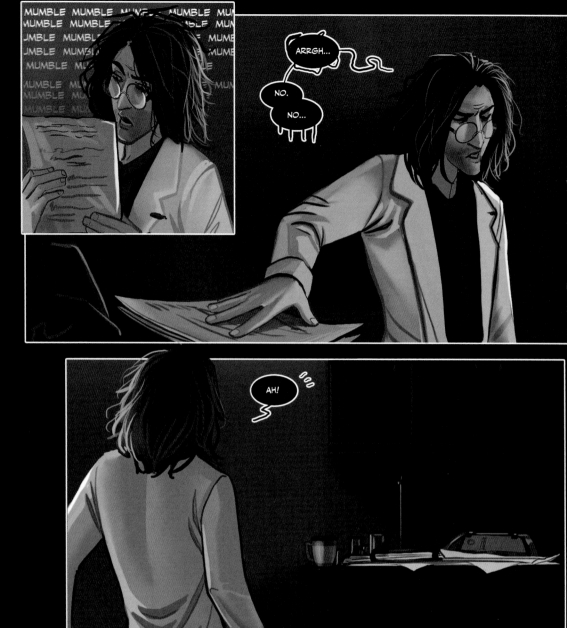

UGH!!
FIT, DAMN IT!
TAP
TAP
TAP
TAP
KHM!
SO...UM...
AREN'T YOU GONNA FOLLOW HIM?
SHOULD I?
WELL--
YOU ARE HIS ASSISTANT, AREN'T YOU?

DOCTOR, WAIT!!
TAK
TAK
TAK
HUH?
DID HE LEAVE ALREADY?
BOSS?
AH!

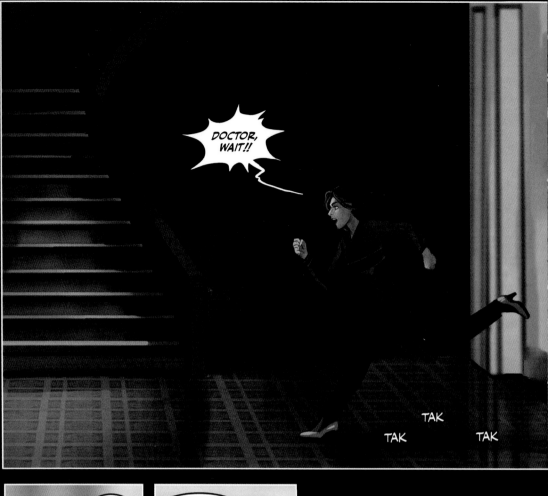

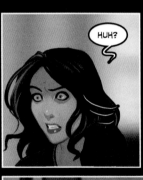

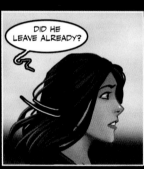

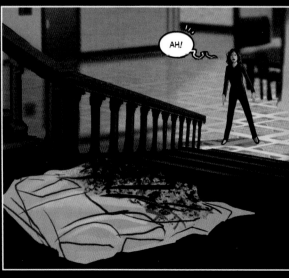

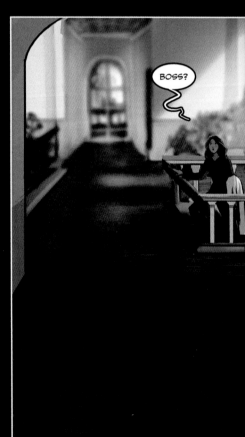

I GUESS HE DID...
WELL THAT'S JUST GREAT!!
"AREN'T YOU GONNA FOLLOW HIM???
YOU ARE HIS ASSISTANT AREN'T YOU???"
DO I LOOK LIKE I KNOW WHAT I'M DOING??
AND WHY AM I STILL HOLDING THIS...
EWWW!

DROP
SIGH...
MIGHT AS WELL GO TO--
THUNK!
?
UGH.
I SHOULD CHANGE OUT OF THIS ONE TOO...
WHAM
!!!
OH. BOSS? UM...
B-BOSS?
THIS JOB BETTER BE WORTH ALL THIS TRAUMA.

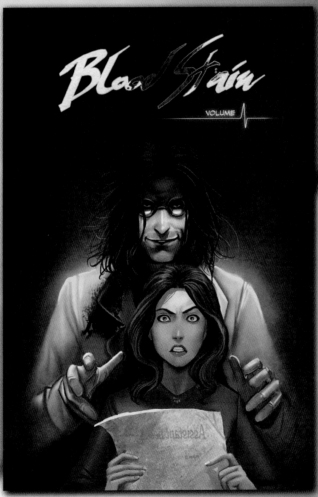

VOLUME 1
DIAMOND CODE:
OCT150604

Blood Stain
VOLUME
LINDA SEJIC
Blood Stain
VOLUME
VOLUME 2
DIAMOND CODE:
JUN160704
VOLUME 3
DIAMOND CODE:
AUG170621
ON SALE NOW!

YISHAN LI + MATT HAWKINS + JENNI CHEUNG
Sugar™
JULY 2018

LOU'S DINER
LOU'S

JULIA

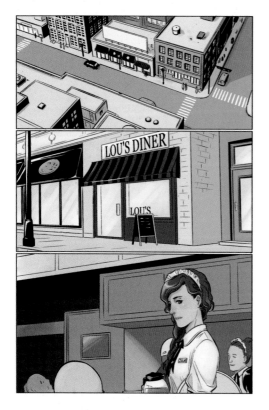

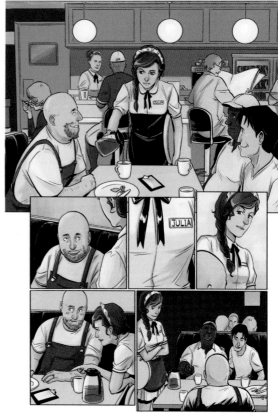

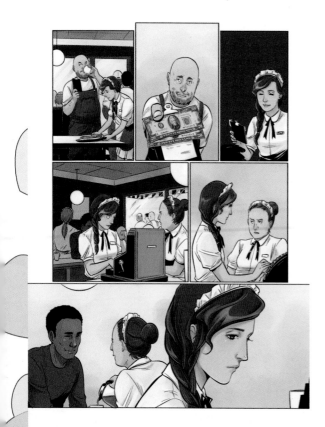

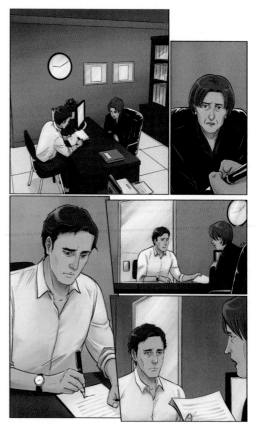

TOTAL:

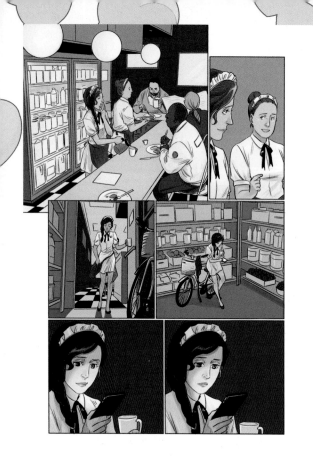

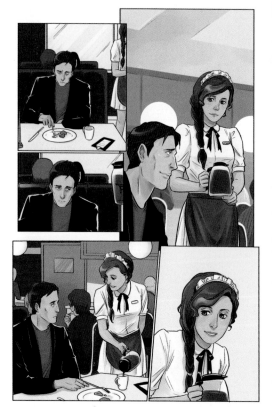

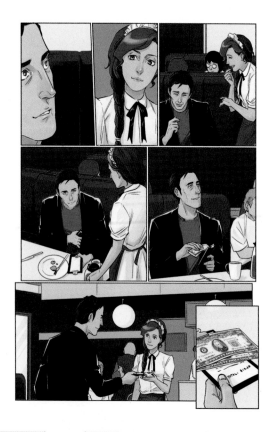

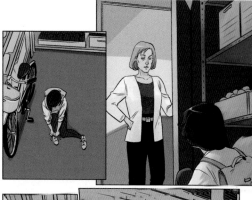

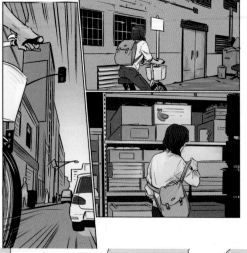

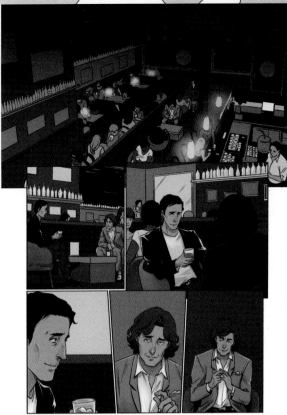

MOM
TUITION FEE NOTICE

ACCOUNT BALANCE
$ 108.27
ENTER AMOUNT
$ 100.00
SENT
NEW BALANCE
$ 8.27
3:30 PM

Cheerios

Vixens bar

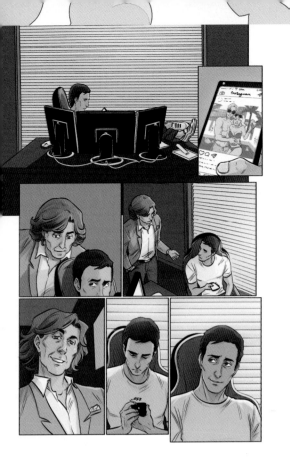

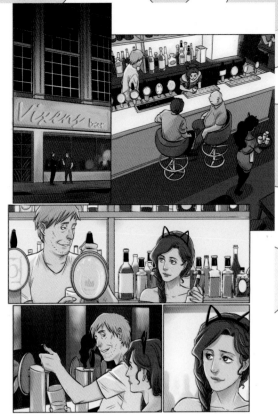

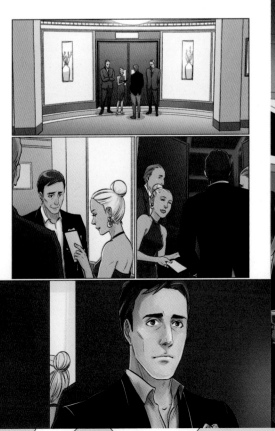

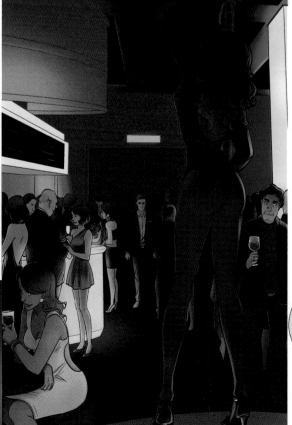

Vixens

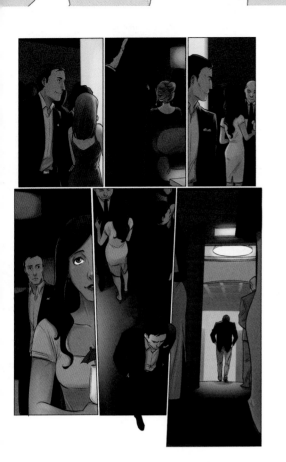

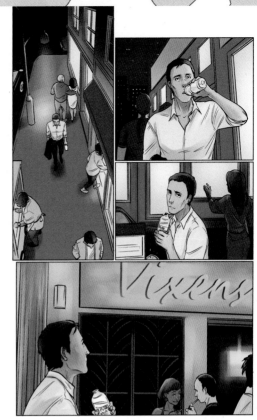

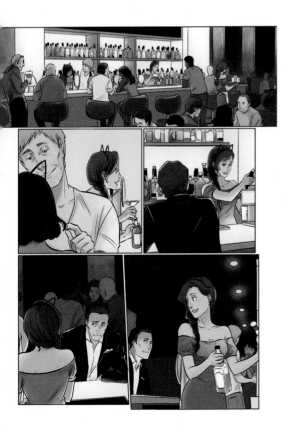

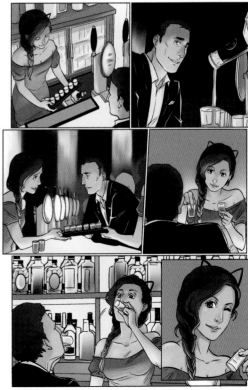

SEX ED

Welcome to my inaugural Sex Ed column! For those of you new to my books I write some sort of column or "extra material" in the back of every book I do. For THINK TANK it's **"Science Class"**, THE TITHE is **"Sunday School"** and so on. I was going to call this "Sex Class" but Vince in our office tossed out **"Sex Ed"** and it stuck. I do a lot of research for every project and this was no exception. We'll get into more of that later. You don't have to read this afterword to get the story, it's just something extra I add to try to create more value for you as a reader and to share what I learned in the writing process.

SUNSTONE

The only reason this book exists is because of the success of Stjepan Sejic's SUNSTONE. Stjepan Sejic started out with Top Cow many years ago as a colorist over Tyler Kirkham's work. Tyler had befriended him online and we started working with him out of that friendship. Sejic took over WITCHBLADE and did eighty issues or so and then did a long run on APHRODITE IX and IXTH GENERATION that I wrote. I was "friendly" with him while he was doing WITCHBLADE when we began working directly together creatively. I can now safely count him and his wife as real friends...and I'd do just about anything for them. They're amazing people.

It was at some point in his WITCHBLADE/APHRODITE IX runs he started doing SUNSTONE as a strip he posted on his DeviantArt account (**https://shiniez.deviantart.com**) as a free webcomic. When I asked him about it he said he needed to do something

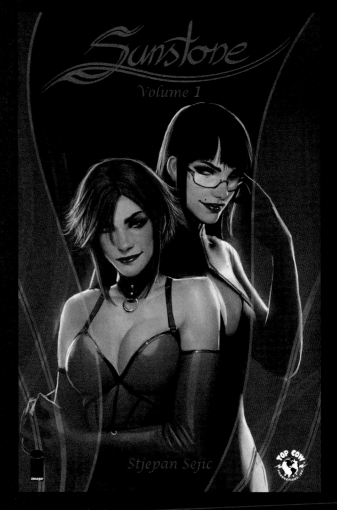

different to juice him creatively. At the time, I thought nothing about it. When I looked at it, it was cool, slice-of life material about two lesbian girls into S&M and there was sex and actual nudity in it. WHOA! In my reading of it though, it didn't feel sexist, it was sexy. There's a massive difference and I try to explain that to some people and they can't seem to grasp the difference. It was a sex positive look at an alternate lifestyle.

Flash forward a few years and Stjepan asked me if we'd sell print editions of SUNSTONE. I was REALLY hesitant. We'd been trying for years and years to get away from the perception of our content from the 90s bad girl era and this was a comic strip he was GIVING AWAY FOR FREE already. Why would anyone buy it? I thought about it and decided we'd do it... simply because Sejic wanted us to. I really thought it wouldn't sell all that well. Not only was I wrong, I was INSANELY wrong. I've never been happier to be wrong. Let me put it in perspective: SUNSTONE has sold more copies of the collected editions than any other book in Top Cow history...and that includes the heyday of the early 90s.